THREADS OF WAR

THREAD WITCH BOOK 3

ALSO BY RICHARD FIERCE

DRAGON RIDERS OF OSNEN

Trial by Sorcery
A Bond of Flame
The Warrior's Call
The Coin of Souls
Wings of Terror
Eyes of Stone
Tooth and Claw
The Servant of Souls
Smoke and Shadow
The Dark Rider
The Song of Bones
Sword and Crown
Tides of Darkness
Wrath and Ruin
Tomb of Oaths

MARKED BY THE DRAGON

Curse of the Dragon
Scale of the Dragon
Egg of the Dragon
Call of the Dragon
Wrath of the Dragon
Sacrifice of the Dragon

THREADS OF WAR

THREAD WITCH BOOK 3

RICHARD FIERCE

Dragonfire Press

Print ISBN: 979-8-89631-091-4

To my readers.
Thank you for everything.

THREAD WITCH
3
THREADS
OF WAR
RICHARD FIERCE

CHAPTER 1
Amara

The needle in her hand was carved from bone. Not bleached white, but the sickly yellow-gray of something that had been buried too long in poisoned earth. It moved through flesh easily, each stitch binding skin to skin with threads that gleamed like silver mercury.

Not fabric, she realized with growing horror. *I'm stitching flesh.*

The woman beneath her needle didn't scream. Her eyes held an emptiness that came from having her voice stripped away, consciousness compressed into a silence she'd never chosen. But her mouth moved soundlessly around words that might have been pleas or prayers, while tears streamed down cheeks that bore the ritual scarification of someone who'd once served the Bone Cloister.

"You cannot cut what you are," whispered a voice that carried layers—young and old, male and female, human and something else entirely. "You are the seam. The thread. The needle."

The Weaver of Bone stood behind her in the dream, his presence radiating satisfaction as he watched her work. Not forcing her movements, not compelling her compliance, but simply observing as she bound living flesh.

"This is what you were made for," he continued. "Not preservation of what was, but creation of what must be. The old distinctions—life, death, willing, unwilling—are limitations that your gift can transcend."

Amara tried to drop the needle, to step away from the table where the anonymous woman lay bound by her own stitching. But her hands moved independently of conscious will, guided by understanding that felt truer than anything she'd learned through years of careful practice.

The thread turned to bone in her fingers, gleaming white strands that pulsed with their own rhythm as they wove flesh into patterns that had never existed in nature. Beautiful, in their way. Perfect, according to standards that had nothing to do with consent or mercy or individual choice.

This is what I could become, she understood with crystalline clarity. *Not someone violated against her will, but a willing participant embracing darkness because it promises heights that virtue could never reach.*

Amara jolted upright in her bedroll, heart hammering against her ribs while sweat soaked the fabric that clung to her trembling form. Around her, the forest clearing where they'd made camp remained peaceful. Early dawn light filtered through the leaves, and birds were beginning their morning songs. There was no sign of danger anywhere.

But her hands still tingled with the memory of the bone needle moving through yielding flesh, while the silver scars along her arms pulsed. *Just a dream,* she told herself, flexing fingers that felt foreign despite belonging to her own body. *Nothing more than stress and exhaustion manifesting as a nightmare.*

But the lie tasted hollow even as she formed it. The soul-link she'd forged with the Weaver of Bone during their final confrontation had created a connection—not just a magical bond, but something that touched the essence of who she was becoming.

Each night brought new dreams, new visions of what her gift could accomplish if she stopped limiting herself. The Weaver didn't force or compel—he simply showed her possibilities, let her experience what it felt like to work without moral restrictions or artificial constraints.

And each morning, she woke with growing certainty that some part of her wanted to accept what he offered.

Caedric sat beside their small fire, tending flames that painted his angular features in shades of gold and amber. He looked up when she approached, his pale eyes reflecting concern that had become his default expression whenever he observed her too closely.

"Morning," he said, his voice steady as a lighthouse beam cutting through the nightmares that still ebbed within her. "Sleep well?"

The question was casual, carefully neutral, but she caught undertones that suggested he'd noticed her restlessness. How could he not, when she woke gasping most nights, when her scars blazed with light that painted their camp in silver patterns that had nothing to do with normal fire?

"Well enough," she lied, accepting the waterskin he offered. "Just... strange dreams. Nothing worth discussing."

For a moment their hands nearly brushed as she took the water, but she pulled away before contact could be made. Not from revulsion or fear, but from understanding that touch would reveal truths she wasn't ready to admit. That, and the tether that bound her to the Weaver carried frequencies that might contaminate anyone who got too close to what she was becoming.

Caedric's expression flickered with something that might have been hurt before professional neutrality reasserted itself. He'd learned to read her moods over weeks of shared flight, had probably noticed the patterns she thought she'd hidden successfully.

But he didn't press, didn't demand explanations she couldn't provide without revealing how precarious her grip on her identity had become. He just nodded and returned his attention to the fire, offering the kind of respectful distance that felt like kindness and torture in equal measure.

He suspects something is wrong, she realized. *But he's waiting for me to trust him with the truth I'm hiding.*

The problem was that trust required the hope she might still be worth saving, and hope felt increasingly naive with each dream she had.

———— ◆ ————

They spread the prophecy tapestry on ground still damp with morning dew, its ancient patterns catching the light of dawn. Despite its fragmented condition—torn during their escape from the Bone Cloister, stained with blood and worse substances—the map worked into its foundation remained clear enough to guide their journey.

Three cities glowed with gold-threaded runes that pulsed like heartbeats, their locations revealing settlements that existed beyond Amara's knowledge. They had slipped through the cracks of official maps and Guild records not through insignificance, but through deliberate obscurity—settlements where practitioners of the old ways had cultivated the art of remaining unremarkable to those who might seek to control them.

"Eryndale," she said, tracing the first marker with a fingertip that tingled at contact with the supernatural cartography. "The others are Millbrook and Thornhaven. All of them marked for something the cult considered significant enough to weave into their greatest working."

"You think they'll listen to warnings from strangers?" Caedric asked, studying the ancient textile. "Most independent communities become independent precisely because they don't trust outside authority."

"Their cities won't listen," Amara agreed, rolling the tapestry carefully to avoid further damage to its delicate patterns. "But the people will. Individuals who understand that survival sometimes requires cooperation with those who share common enemies."

The distinction felt crucial, though she couldn't articulate why. Cities were abstractions, political entities that existed in documents and official proclamations. But people were real, immediate, flesh-and-blood individuals who made their own decisions, regardless of what powers claimed to speak in their name.

And people, she was beginning to understand, were what truly mattered in wars that touched both personal and cosmic stakes.

The voice came as they prepared to break camp, faint as a whisper carried on the wind that barely stirred the forest leaves. Not audible in the normal sense—no vibrations in the air, no sound that normal hearing could detect. But present nonetheless, weaving itself between her thoughts like thread through the warp and weft of her mind.

Sister. Daughter. Apprentice yet to acknowledge her calling.

The words carried cadences she recognized despite trying to forget them. The Weaver's layered voice, made from the accumulated identities he'd claimed through centuries of careful harvesting, speaking through a connection that grew stronger rather than weaker with each passing day.

Come home. The Cloister waits. Your destiny waits. Why do you fight what you were made to become?

Her silver scars blazed to life, tracing fiery patterns along her forearms as they answered some unheard call that spoke to their very essence. Not the gentle warmth she'd associated with her gift, but a burning intensity.

Without conscious thought, Amara drew her belt knife and carved a quick sigil into her palm—a technique she'd learned from observing Wraithstitcher methods, though applied in reverse. Not binding corruption, but disrupting it, severing the pathways through which unwanted influence might flow.

Blood welled from the shallow cut while the voice faded to a barely perceptible murmur, its insistence muffled by pain that served as a barrier between her and the Weaver.

"What's wrong?" Caedric's voice cut through the moment's disorientation, sharp with concern that had shifted toward alarm. "Your hand—you're bleeding."

"Nothing," she said quickly, wrapping the cut in strip of cloth that absorbed the red evidence of her growing desperation. "Just... caught it on a thorn. Clumsy."

But his pale eyes had seen too much to accept such casual dismissal. His gaze lingered on her hand, on the precise angles of the cut that formed a pattern too deliberate for mishap, too familiar to anyone trained to recognize forbidden symbols. This wasn't the gentle preservation magic she'd shown him— this was something else entirely.

"Amara." His voice was firm with authority. "What aren't you telling me?"

The question hung between them, sharp with implications that could reshape everything they'd built together. He deserved truth—had earned it through his loyalty that went beyond duty, protection that risked his own safety for her freedom.

But truth felt like a weapon pointed at the only person who'd chosen to stand beside her when every other authority sought to claim or destroy her gifts. How could she explain that the woman he'd risked everything to save was slowly being consumed by a connection to everything he'd sworn to oppose?

"I'm fine," she said finally. "Ready to travel?"

———◆———

Eryndale lay two days' ride through forest paths that wound between tall, ancient trees, their massive trunks bearing scars from conflicts that had shaped the land before Guild authority imposed its particular version of order. The settlement thrived in obscurity, invisible to the Guild not through magic or secrecy, but because the powerful rarely bothered looking at what they deemed insignificant.

Hoofbeats marked their progress toward Eryndale, each step bringing Amara closer to a confrontation she dreaded—not with enemies, but with the weight of expectations. Despite her attempts to leave no trace of herself in the world, stories had taken root like stubborn weeds, spreading her name in whispers that grew more elaborate with each retelling.

The thread-witch. The woman who defied Guild and cult alike.

She'd heard the whispers in the last village they'd passed through, seen the way common folk looked at her with a mixture of hope and fear that spoke of legends already taking shape around deeds she'd never intended to become symbolic. They wanted her to be something more than an individual struggling with gifts she'd never asked to possess—wanted her to become a banner they could rally behind in struggles against forces too large for any single person to face.

But she'd never wanted to be a symbol or a savior, had never sought leadership that would make her responsible for others' hopes and dreams. The very idea of people looking to her for salvation felt like a trap that would destroy what remained of her.

I don't need to be a savior, she thought, watching the road ahead wind toward the horizon. *I just need to make sure no one else becomes me.*

Salvation required wisdom she didn't possess, strength she hadn't developed, certainty about right and wrong that grew more elusive with each dream. But prevention was simpler, more concrete. Warning people about dangers that stalked them from the shadows, giving them knowledge that might help them make informed choices about their own survival.

Whether that would be enough to satisfy the destiny the tether seemed determined to impose remained to be seen. But for now, riding toward communities that might listen to warnings from strangers, it felt like a purpose that could sustain her despite the growing certainty that her time as an individual agent was running out.

Behind them, the forest's shadows seemed to whisper with voices that carried the sounds of bone and ash. The Weaver's influence followed wherever she went, patient as death. But ahead lay people who deserved the chance to choose their own paths rather than accepting what others sought to impose.

And that, perhaps, was reason enough to continue fighting whatever she was becoming, at least until the choice was no longer hers to make.

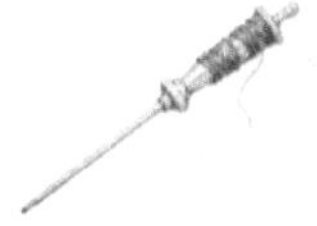

CHAPTER 2
Caedric

The banners hanging from Eryndale's gates were wrong.

Caedric reined in his horse at the forest's edge, studying the familiar crimson and gold that had once represented order and protection in his mind. Now they looked like bloodstains against the pale stone walls, marking territory claimed through fear rather than earned through service.

The Sigil of Purity gleamed from the main gatehouse—a new addition that made his stomach clench with recognition. The stylized flame consuming a tangle of threads wasn't just Guild heraldry. It was the mark of the Hemlock Circle, specifically an elite purification unit that specialized in identifying and eliminating what they termed "corrupted threadlines."

They aren't just controlling the city, he realized, counting the patrol patterns with professional assessment. *They're expecting her.*

"Something's wrong," Amara said, her voice barely above a whisper as she studied the scene ahead. "There are too many of them for a standard occupation."

The observation was accurate. What should have been a handful of Guild representatives maintaining nominal authority had become a full military presence. Guard towers that hadn't existed a season ago now stood like sentinels, while patrols moved in formations designed to discourage unauthorized entry.

"It's a trap," Caedric said simply. "But not for anyone they can identify by sight. They're casting wide nets, hoping to catch rumors."

He'd seen similar deployments during his years with the Hemlock Circle—not searches for specific individuals, but campaigns to eliminate entire categories of threat. The kind of thorough purification that left communities cleansed of whatever independence they'd once possessed.

A banner caught his attention as it shifted in the afternoon breeze, revealing the insignia of the Thirteenth Company, his old unit, marked by the intertwined serpent and flame that had once decorated his own robes.

For a moment, muscle memory nearly made him straighten in the saddle, ready to report to commanders who'd shaped his understanding of duty and honor. Men who'd taught him that sacrifice for the greater good was the highest calling any individual could embrace.

Brothers who'd kill me without hesitation now, he reminded himself, though the thought carried more sadness than bitterness. *Because I chose her over everything they taught me to value.*

"Caedric?" Amara's voice held concern that made him realize he'd been staring too long at symbols from a life he'd abandoned. "Are you all right?"

"Just remembering a thread I cut," he said, turning his attention away from the banner. "We'll need another way in."

———◆———

His contact found them in a grove of standing stones, ancient markers where the old agreements between communities had been sealed with blood and thread. Tallis emerged from the shadows, his movements guarded.

"Caedric," he said. "The Hemlock deserter who stole a Guild asset and vanished into legend."

"The asset has a name," Caedric replied, hand moving to the hilt of his thread-cutter. "And she's under my protection."

"Peace." Tallis raised both hands in a gesture of neutrality. "I meant no insult. The stories that reached us were... incomplete. We knew only that someone had defied the Guild's claim on the thread-witch, not who or why."

Thread-Witch. The title had spread faster than wildfire, transforming Amara from an individual into a symbol whether she wanted the transformation or not. He'd heard it whispered in taverns, seen it carved into tree bark along the roads they'd traveled, felt its weight in the way people looked at her with hope and fear in equal measure.

"I'm not a witch," Amara said quietly. "I'm just someone trying to warn people about dangers they can't see."

Tallis studied her with interest that held layers—not the calculating assessment of someone weighing an advantage, but the careful attention of a scholar encountering a text he'd only heard described. "Perhaps. But the Guild is executing citizens for whispering your name, and rumors have power whether we acknowledge them or not."

Executions for rumors meant the Guild had moved beyond their usual methods of control, abandoning legal frameworks in favor of pure intimidation.

"How many?" Caedric asked.

"Seventeen confirmed in the past week," Tallis replied. "All accused of spreading seditious narratives about resistance to Guild authority. The Hemlock Circle has convinced the local commander that preventing revolution requires eliminating the stories that might inspire it."

Seventeen people dead for speaking a name. The number felt like a weight settling around Caedric's shoulders, responsibility for consequences that had grown far beyond anything they'd intended when they'd fled the Guild Hall together.

She never wanted this, he thought, watching Amara's face pale as she absorbed the implications. *Never wanted her freedom to cost other people their lives.*

"There's a way through the siege lines," Tallis continued. "Hidden paths the old stitchers used to move materials between communities without paying taxes. But they're dangerous in their own way."

"More dangerous than walking through the front gate?" Amara asked.

"Different kinds of danger," Tallis said. "The tunnels remember everything that passed through them. Stories, emotions… the weight of centuries of secrets. Some people emerge unchanged. Others… don't emerge as themselves."

The entrance lay concealed beneath a tangle of thornvines that had grown wild over what appeared to be natural stone formations. But as Tallis moved aside the living camouflage, carved steps became visible, descending into darkness.

"The memory passages," he explained, producing a lamp that burned with threads of gold light. "Built by the first stitchers who settled this region, back when the Guild was nothing more than a few ambitious theorists arguing about proper technique."

The steps led down into chambers carved from living rock, their walls covered with threadwork patterns that seemed to shift and flow in the lamplight. Not decorative designs, but actual narratives woven into the stone through methods that hadn't been used since the Guild standardized all magical practices according to their interpretation of proper form.

"What are they?" Amara asked, running her fingers along threads that gleamed like metal and felt warm to the touch.

"Stories," Tallis replied. "Every significant event that shaped this community, preserved in the literal fabric of their foundation. Birth records, trade agreements, marriage contracts, death songs. The kind of comprehensive record-keeping that makes communities immortal."

Caedric studied the patterns more closely, recognizing techniques from his Guild training but applied with creativity that had been discouraged by the time he'd learned them. These weren't just records—they were living memory, threads that carried the emotional weight of the experiences they preserved.

One section caught his attention, its patterns more complex than the surrounding work. The threads formed images that moved as he watched, depicting events that felt familiar despite their obvious antiquity. Guild banners, but different somehow. Cleaner, carrying symbols that spoke of protection.

"The founding of the Guild," Amara observed, following his gaze to the moving tapestry. "But they look... different."

"They were," Tallis said. "The original Guilds were protector organizations, formed to defend independent practitioners from the imperial standardization campaigns. They fought *for* community autonomy, not against it."

Everything he'd been taught about Guild history, about the noble calling that had shaped his understanding of duty and service, had been built on carefully edited narratives that excluded inconvenient truths.

How many stories did the Guild unweave to stitch their power? he wondered, studying images that showed his former colleagues' predecessors standing with communities rather than above them.

The passage curved deeper into the earth, following routes that seemed to spiral toward some central purpose. Other chambers branched off the main tunnel, each one filled with its own collection of preserved experiences, but they stayed on the direct path that Tallis indicated would bring them up beneath Eryndale's market district.

As they walked, Caedric found himself thinking about the way stories shaped reality whether people realized it or not. The Guild had built their authority on controlled versions of history, presenting themselves as the natural inheritors of tradition while systematically eliminating the evidence of alternatives.

But here, in chambers that predated Guild influence, different stories survived. Stories that suggested other possibilities, other ways of understanding the relationship between individual gift and community need.

She's not just threatening their control, he realized, watching Amara navigate the memory-threaded passages. *She's proving that their version of history isn't the only one that matters.*

They emerged through a concealed entrance that placed them in the heart of Eryndale's abandoned weaver market, surrounded by stalls that had once housed the independent artisans who'd made the city famous throughout the region. Now the empty booths stood like tombstones, marking the death of a community culture that had thrived for generations before Guild authority arrived to impose its version of order.

The silence felt unnatural in a space designed for commerce and conversation, but as they stepped into the central square, someone began humming. A simple melody, the kind of song that accompanied repetitive tasks, but it carried harmonies that spoke of a time long forgotten.

Another voice joined the first, then another. The tune spread through the square as people emerged from doorways and side streets, not approaching but simply taking their places in a gathering that felt spontaneous and inevitable at the same time.

Caedric's hand moved to his thread-cutter, his instincts recognizing the potential for the crowd's dynamics to shift from peaceful to dangerous. But no weapons appeared among the gathering citizens, no aggressive gestures or hostile intent. They simply stood and sang, creating something that felt like a ceremony without the formal structure.

They're not afraid, he realized with growing amazement. *They're welcoming her.*

The song ended, leaving silence that held weight and expectation. Then a child stepped forward—a girl perhaps ten years old, with the careful posture of someone who'd been chosen for an important task. In her hands she carried something wrapped in clean cloth, small enough to fit in her palms.

"For the thread-witch," she said, her young voice carrying clearly in the quiet square. "From the stitchers who remember what we were before they told us what we should become."

Amara knelt to accept the gift, unwrapping the cloth to reveal a small sigil worked in threads that caught the afternoon light. A stylized flame rising above a loom, simple in design but complex in execution, created with techniques that spoke of skill passed down through generations.

"I'm not who you think I am," Amara said softly, holding the sigil with careful reverence. "I'm not the answer to the questions you're carrying."

"You're exactly who we hoped you'd be," replied a voice from the crowd, an older woman whose hands bore the calluses of decades spent working thread into meaning. "Someone who chose her own path instead of accepting what others decided was best for her."

Caedric studied the faces around them, seeing hope that had found focus, community that had discovered purpose in the simple act of standing together rather than bowing separately.

She's not leading a rebellion, he realized. *She's becoming one.*

The realization should have terrified him—rebellion meant war, and war meant casualties among people who deserved protection rather than sacrifice. But watching Amara accept their gift with the grace that acknowledged both honor and burden, he felt something else entirely.

Pride. Not in conquest or victory, but in the simple courage required to remain human in circumstances designed to strip away everything that made humanity worth preserving.

Whatever came next, whatever forces gathered against them, whatever prices would be demanded from all of them—he would stand beside her. He would protect what mattered most in a world that seemed determined to destroy anything beautiful or free.

The crowd began to disperse, melting back into doorways and side streets, but their message had been delivered, their position made clear. Eryndale would not bow willingly to Guild authority, and the thread-witch had allies who would stand with her when the final accounting came.

The revolution had found its banner, and Caedric had chosen his side.

CHAPTER 3
Amara

Pain woke her from dreamless sleep—not the sharp bite of injury, but something deeper. A burning that spread through her chest and down her left arm like molten silver poured beneath her skin, following pathways that had nothing to do with blood or breath.

Amara rolled from her bedroll in the safehouse beneath the apothecary, biting back a gasp that might wake Caedric where he slept near the door. The pain pulsed in rhythm with her heartbeat, but wrong somehow, as if something else had synchronized itself to her body's natural cadences.

Threadburn, she recognized, though this felt different from the familiar ache that came from overextending her gift. This burned like corruption, like poison working its way through her veins.

She stumbled toward the cracked mirror that hung above a basin of water, needing to see what was happening to her body. Her reflection looked normal at first—fair skin, dark hair tangled from restless sleep, silver scars still faintly visible along her arms.

Then the pain flared again, and she saw them.

White lines etched themselves beneath her skin like ink dropped into clear water, spreading in patterns that resembled runes but felt alien to everything she understood about threadwork. Not the flowing curves of traditional stitching, but angular symbols that cut through her flesh with geometric precision.

Bone runes, she realized with growing horror. The Weaver's mark, written in her very flesh, mapping across her body like an unfinished garment waiting to be completed.

Without conscious thought, she reached for her traveling pack and pulled out a needle and thread, desperate to create something—anything—that might serve as a barrier against the force was rewriting her nature. A simple warding sigil stitched into her shawl, protective patterns her grandmother had taught her.

But the thread wouldn't obey.

It twisted in her fingers like something alive, coiling and uncoiling like a living thing that refused to touch the cloth. When she tried to force the stitching, the thread began to whisper—not words, but sounds that carried the texture of bone scraping against stone, of graves being dug in frozen earth.

"You will stitch from bone. That is what you were made for."

The voice came from everywhere and nowhere, threading through her consciousness. Not spoken aloud, but present in the space between heartbeats, in the pause between one breath and the next.

"Why do you fight what you are becoming? Why cling to limitations that were never meant to contain gifts such as yours?"

"Because *I* choose what I become," she whispered to the mirror, watching the white runes pulse beneath skin that no longer felt entirely her own. "Because some things are too dangerous to want."

Laughter answered her—not cruel, but genuinely amused, echoing with the weary patience of one who had watched a thousand souls struggle against their destiny only to surrender in the end.

"Choice is an illusion. You can accept your nature with grace, or be dragged to the same destination kicking and screaming. But you will arrive regardless."

The thread in her hands began to smoke, releasing vapors that smelled of burial earth and old bones. She dropped it, watching the fibers curl and blacken as they touched the floor, leaving stains that looked disturbingly like dried blood.

Without thinking, she drew the belt knife and carved a quick line across her palm—not deep enough to cause permanent damage, but sharp enough to produce pain that felt like her own choice rather than something imposed on her.

Blood welled from the cut, red and warm and reassuringly human. For a moment, the bone runes beneath her skin faded, their ghostly light dimmed by pain that belonged entirely to her.

At least I can still choose to hurt, she thought, pressing cloth against the wound to stop the bleeding. *At least some parts of me are still mine to control.*

But even as she formed the thought, she wondered how long that would remain true.

"What's happening to you?"

Caedric's voice cut through her attempt to slip quietly back to her bedroll, sharp with concern that had shifted toward alarm. He stood in the doorway, pale eyes taking in details she'd hoped to hide—the bloodstained cloth wrapped around her hand, the way she held herself like someone trying not to flinch.

"Nothing," she said quickly. "Just couldn't sleep. Cut myself on something in the dark."

His gaze moved to the scattered remains of thread that still smoldered near the mirror, to the way her left arm trembled like a puppet with tangled strings.

"Amara." His tone was stern but filled with worry. "You know you can tell me anything. *Anything.*"

The words hung between them. He deserved honesty, had more than earned it. But how could she tell him that his oath to shield her meant nothing when the very magic he'd spent his life hunting was now threading itself through her veins, remaking her from within?

"You said you'd protect me," she said instead, words coming out sharper than she'd intended. "What happens when you can't protect others from me?"

She watched his expression shift from concern to understanding to something that might have been grief, as if he'd been hoping she wouldn't voice the fears that had been growing in his own mind.

For a long moment, he was silent. When he finally answered, his words came heavy with resignation, not warning.

"Then I will stand in your path. If I must."

The words shook her more than anger would have, more than promises or platitudes about finding solutions. He wasn't offering false comfort or denying the possibility that she might become something that needed to be stopped.

He was simply promising that when that moment came—if it came—she wouldn't face it alone.

Even if it means standing against me, she realized. *Even if it costs him everything he's fought to protect.*

Whatever she was becoming, however the tether changed her, Caedric would be there to remind her of who she'd been before the Weaver claimed pieces of her soul.

———◆———

The hidden archive lay deeper beneath the apothecary than she'd expected, reached through passages that wound between natural caverns and carved chambers. Tallis led them through spaces that felt older than the building above, older perhaps than the city itself.

"The original practitioners," he explained, his lamp casting shadows that danced across walls lined with alcoves filled with scrolls and artifacts. "They understood that some knowledge was too dangerous for general access, but too valuable to lose entirely."

The collection was unlike anything Amara had seen. Scrolls wrapped in silk that seemed to shift color in the lamplight, containing techniques for working with thread types that had been banned for generations. Memory thread that could preserve experiences as vividly as lived reality. Dream thread that could carry messages through sleeping minds. Decay thread that could accelerate or slow the passage of time through organic matter.

And in a place of honor at the archive's center, displayed on a pedestal carved from a single piece of black stone, sat something that made her breath catch in her throat.

The Bone Spindle.

It looked innocent enough at first glance—just an ancient tool for drawing fiber into thread, worn smooth by countless hands over centuries of use. But as she studied it more closely, something about the spindle's proportions whispered of unnatural origins. The shaft was carved from bone that had never belonged to any natural creature, while the whorl was carved from a stone so dark it drank the lamplight, leaving a void where illumination should have been.

A weaving tool of the first Deathstitchers, she realized, remembering fragments of the history her grandmother had taught her. The ancient craftsmen had fashioned it to spin thread from the whispers of the dying.

The spindle called to her with a pull that felt like gravity, like the tide, like the inevitable draw of breath following breath. Not demanding or commanding, but simply... waiting, offering possibilities that normal tools could never provide.

She took a step toward the pedestal before catching herself.

"Don't let curiosity lead you to your cage," Caedric warned, his voice strained as he recognized the hunger in her eyes. "Some doors open easily but close with considerable difficulty."

He's right, she told herself, forcing her attention away from the artifact that whispered of answers to questions she hadn't yet found the words to ask. *I'm already connected to forces I can't control. I don't need to invite more corruption.*

But part of her—a growing part— wondered what she might accomplish with tools designed for working beyond the boundaries that confined normal threadwork. What warnings she might weave, what protections she might create, what changes she might implement if she stopped limiting herself to techniques that pretended death was separate from life. An idea came to her.

"A Whisper Loom," she said, speaking it aloud. "We could connect these archives, create a network that carries messages between communities faster than any Guild courier."

Tallis looked up from the scroll he'd been examining, interest sharp in his eyes. "Thread-carried communication across distances? The theory is sound, but the practical considerations—"

"Memory thread," she continued, the concept maturing with each word. "Woven with techniques that embed experience rather than just information. And not warnings about what's coming, but actual understanding of what to expect."

The others in the archive began to gather around her, drawn by confidence that surprised even her with its strength. She'd never thought of herself as a leader, had never sought the kind of authority that made people look to her for direction and inspiration.

But as she outlined the possibilities—hidden communication routes, early warning systems, ways to coordinate resistance across regions—she watched their expressions shift from interest to excitement to something approaching devotion.

They're seeing me as the answer, she realized. *Not just to immediate problems, but to the larger questions about how to survive in a world that wants to crush anything beautiful or free.*

The recognition should have pleased her, but instead it felt like weight settling around her shoulders. How could she guide others when she couldn't trust her own motivations? How could she offer leadership when she wasn't certain she'd still be herself by tomorrow morning?

What kind of leader bleeds in secret? she wondered, touching the cloth that still covered the cut on her palm. *What kind of savior needs saving from herself?*

But the work needed doing, and there was no one else positioned to do it. Whatever she was becoming, whatever the tether might cost her, people were depending on warnings that could save their lives and communities that deserved the chance to choose their own responses to the forces gathering against them.

————◆————

That night, Caedric positioned himself near the door with his thread-cutter within easy reach, his body language speaking of readiness for threats that might come from any direction. Including, she realized, from her.

The knowledge should have hurt, but instead it felt like kindness. He wasn't pretending the danger didn't exist, he was simply preparing to do whatever became necessary, accepting the responsibility for choices that might be forced upon them both.

Amara lay on her bedroll staring at the ceiling, too aware of the bone runes that pulsed faintly beneath her skin to risk the dreams that had been growing more vivid with each passing night. Instead, she began stitching with her fingers—not thread, but memory.

Patterns that recalled her grandmother's gentle hands teaching basic techniques, the warmth of hearth fire during long winter evenings, the simple satisfaction of creating something beautiful and useful with nothing more than patience and skill.

Before I knew my gift was dangerous, she thought, tracing invisible designs in the air above her chest. *Before I understood that some forms of power come with prices too high for any individual to pay.*

But even as she worked the comforting memories, she could feel other patterns trying to assert themselves. Designs that would work better with bone needles rather than steel ones, techniques that could accomplish in minutes what normal threadwork required hours to achieve.

You will stitch from bone, the voice whispered from between conscious thoughts. *That is what I made you for.*

He said he'd stand in my path, she reminded herself, watching Caedric's steady breathing in the lamplight. *He never said he'd leave me.* Perhaps that would be enough to help her remember who she'd been before forces beyond her understanding decided who she should become.

Even if the enemy she feared most was the one taking shape beneath her own skin.

CHAPTER 4
Caedric

Dawn had not yet touched the safehouse when Caedric woke to the sound of Amara's restless movements. Not the tossing and turning of ordinary sleep, but something more deliberate—her hands weaving patterns in the air above her chest, fingers tracing designs that glowed faintly in the pre-dawn darkness.

He lay still, watching her work through whatever visions or compulsions drove her increasingly troubled rest. The woman who'd once slept peacefully beside campfires had become someone who fought battles even in unconsciousness, her body responding to threats that existed only to her closed eyes.

She's changing, he observed, studying the subtle alterations that had accrued over the weeks since they'd fled the Guild Hall together. Not just stronger—though the power that radiated from her had grown noticeably—but haunted. Marked by the kind of exhaustion that came from constant vigilance against enemies that couldn't be fought with conventional weapons.

He'd seen that look before, during his years with the Hemlock Circle. Rogue weavers who'd touched forces beyond their understanding, practitioners who'd been corrupted by the very gifts they'd tried to master. The haunted expression of someone hunted from the inside out, fighting battles against aspects of themselves that had been turned into weapons by influences they couldn't escape.

But unlike those previous encounters, he didn't fear her. He feared *for* her.

Those other practitioners had been cases to solve, problems to address through careful application of Guild doctrine and superior force. Threats to be neutralized rather than individuals to be saved.

Amara was... more. She was the choice he'd made when all of his training and every instinct had demanded a different decision.

The proof that some things mattered more than duty or doctrine or the careful calculations that had once defined his understanding of right and wrong.

I once vowed to unravel monsters, he thought, watching her fingers trace patterns that seemed to ease whatever torment plagued her dreams. *Now I shield her from becoming one.*

The commitment felt like stepping off a cliff into darkness, trusting that purpose would provide the strength necessary to survive the impact awaited at the bottom. But it was his choice to make, his path to follow, and he'd walked too far down it to consider turning back now.

———◆———

"Feymont," Tallis said, studying the map they'd spread across the workbench in the hidden archive. "It's three days' ride if you stick to the main roads, five if you use the forest paths. But the Guild has been increasing patrols along all the major routes."

Caedric nodded, marking potential waypoints and alternate roads. But his attention was divided, part of his awareness focused on the other members of the resistance who moved through the archive's chambers.

"You suspect we have a problem," he said quietly, not making it a question.

Tallis glanced up from the map, meeting his gaze. "Information moves too quickly. Routes we thought were secure turn out to be watched. Safe houses that should have remained hidden get raids within days of being used."

"Someone's providing details to the Guild."

"That's my assessment. But we work through compartmentalized knowledge—no individual should have access to enough information to compromise our entire operation." Tallis rolled up the map carefully, his movements betraying the tension that suggested the problem was more personal than tactical. "Either someone's been feeding information for longer than we realized, or the Guild has sources we haven't identified."

Caedric studied the faces of the other resistance members, applying techniques he'd learned during his years as an Unraveler. Not interrogation methods—those required controlled environments and direct confrontation—but the subtler arts of observation that could reveal inconsistencies between what people said and what they actually believed.

"I could help identify the leak," he offered. "My old training included methods for recognizing deception that don't require Guild authority to employ."

For a moment, Tallis looked like he might refuse the offer. Asking a former Guild enforcer to investigate resistance members carried obvious risks, even one who'd demonstrated his commitment by abandoning everything he'd once served.

But practical necessity won out over ideological purity. Too many lives depended on operational security to let personal reservations override effective action.

"Do what you need to do," Tallis said. "But quietly. If there is a traitor, we don't want to alert them to our suspicions."

The technique was simple in principle, complex in execution. Instead of asking direct questions that might reveal his purpose,

Caedric engaged in casual conversations about potential travel routes, mentioning fictional plans and observing how different people responded to information that should have remained confidential.

Most of the resistance members reacted exactly as expected—offering helpful suggestions, warning about hazards they'd heard about, expressing concern for the risks that faced anyone traveling through Guild-controlled territory. Normal responses from people who wanted to help but had no hidden agendas.

But one person's reactions were different.

Garin was young, perhaps twenty years old, with the callused hands of someone who'd learned threadwork through practical apprenticeship rather than formal training. He participated in conversations about resistance activities with appropriate enthusiasm, offered to help with preparations, asked thoughtful questions about tactics and timing.

But when Caedric mentioned the fictional travel plans, Garin's eyes flickered with something that looked like calculation. Not the open concern shown by others, but the careful assessment of someone weighing how to use the information for purposes beyond the current conversation.

Found you, Caedric thought, maintaining casual conversation while planning his next move. The confirmation brought no satisfaction, just the grim recognition that betrayal had taken root even among people who risked their lives for shared principles.

Following Garin through the archive's chambers required skills Caedric had hoped never to use again, techniques for surveillance that reduced human beings to patterns of behavior that could be analyzed and predicted. But the young man's movements confirmed suspicions that conversation had raised.

He moved through the archive like someone mapping its layout for future reference, paying attention to details that had nothing to do with immediate resistance activities. Entry points, guard rotations, the location of important documents and artifacts. The kind of comprehensive assessment that someone would conduct if they were planning to guide others through spaces they'd never seen.

When Garin slipped away from the main group and began tracing symbols into a piece of cloth—not threadwork, but the simple marks used for Guild communication codes—Caedric knew he'd identified their traitor.

The confrontation took place in one of the archive's smaller chambers, far enough from the main areas that their voices wouldn't carry to others. Caedric waited until Garin finished his coded message before stepping out of the shadows, thread-cutter drawn but held low, ready but not immediately threatening.

"Going somewhere?" he asked, nodding toward the cloth that bore Guild communication symbols.

For a moment, Garin looked like he might try to bluff his way through the encounter. But the expression faded quickly, replaced by resignation that suggested he'd been expecting discovery for some time.

"You don't understand," he said, his young voice carrying exhaustion. "They have my sister. My parents. They took them when I first joined the resistance, said they'd be released if I provided information about resistance activities."

"And you believed them?"

Garin's laugh held bitterness that belonged on someone decades older. "I hoped. What else could I do? Let them die for principles they didn't choose, causes they never supported?"

The explanation carried the weight of genuine tragedy—a young man caught between loyalties that couldn't be reconciled, forced to choose between family and community with no option that didn't require betrayal.

Caedric had encountered similar situations during his Guild years, cases where good people made terrible choices because all available alternatives were worse. But understanding the motivation didn't change the threat that treason represented to everyone who depended on secrecy.

"I'm going to give you a choice," he said. "Leave now. Disappear completely, find somewhere the Guild can't reach you, and never contact anyone from here again. Or I'll stop you from sending any more messages."

"You mean you'll kill me." Garin's hand moved toward his belt, where Caedric now noticed the outline of a concealed blade. "Just like the Guild taught you."

"I mean I'll do whatever becomes necessary to protect the people you're endangering."

Garin drew the hidden knife. It wasn't a proper fighting blade, but sharp enough to be dangerous in close quarters. His movements carried desperation rather than skill, the wild energy of someone who'd been cornered with no good options remaining.

"I can't run," he said, raising the weapon with trembling hands. "They'll know I warned you if I disappear. They'll kill my family anyway, just to make an example."

The attack came without further warning, driven by panic rather than the measured precision of a trained fighter. Garin lunged forward with the knife extended, aiming for Caedric's chest in a move that sacrificed defense for the hope of ending the fight with a single strike.

Caedric stepped aside and drew his thread-cutter in one smooth motion, the blade humming with power as it activated. Not just a sword, but a weapon specifically designed to sever the connections that bound life to flesh, memory to mind, identity to consciousness.

The fight lasted perhaps ten seconds. Garin was brave and desperate, but neither quality provided protection against years of training and experience. The thread-cutter opened his throat before he could attempt a second attack, then continued its work by severing the threads that bound his spirit to his body.

Not just death, but complete dissolution. The kind of ending that left no trace for Guild necromancers to question, no memories for truth-readers to extract from fading consciousness.

Caedric knelt beside the body, checking for signs of life that he knew wouldn't exist. The thread-cutter was thorough in its work, designed to prevent the kind of partial death that could be reversed through Guild healing techniques.

I thought I was done killing for causes, he reflected, studying the young face that would never show the wisdom that might have come with age and better choices. *But I will kill for her.*

The realization should have troubled him—another step down a path that led away from everything he'd once believed about honor and duty. But instead it felt like an acceptance of truths that had been growing clearer with each choice he'd made since deciding to stand with Amara.

He wrapped Garin's body in cloth and carried it deeper into the tunnel system, finding a natural crevice that would serve as a burial place. Not because the young man deserved honor, but because leaving evidence would endanger everyone who'd trusted the archive for protection.

The work took most of an hour, and when it was finished, Caedric returned to the main chambers with dirt under his fingernails and the weight of necessary secrets settling around his shoulders.

————◆————

"The Guild has people among the resistance," he told Amara when she asked about his morning absence. "Even among those who should be most committed to opposing them."

It was the truth without being complete—the kind of careful honesty that preserved security while acknowledging the threats they faced. She deserved to know about the dangers that stalked them from unexpected directions, but didn't need the burden of knowing how those dangers had been eliminated.

"How can we trust anyone?" she asked. "If even the people willing to risk their lives for the resistance might be compromised?"

"We trust carefully," he replied. "We share information on a need-to-know basis. We prepare for betrayal without becoming paralyzed by the possibility."

As they gathered their few possessions for departure from Eryndale, preparing to carry warnings to communities that might not welcome the message, Amara stumbled slightly while lifting her pack. Without thinking, she reached out to steady herself, her hand finding his shoulder, her weight leaning against him for a moment.

It was the first time she'd initiated contact since their argument in the hallway, the first gesture that suggested she might still trust him despite the forces that were changing her in ways neither of them fully understood.

Caedric said nothing, but his hand moved to her back, fingers spreading across fabric that covered skin he could feel growing warm beneath his palm. The contact lasted longer than strictly necessary, a moment of connection that acknowledged everything they couldn't say about the choices they'd made and the prices those choices continued to demand.

That night, alone in the darkness of his bedroll while others slept, Caedric worked by the light of a single candle to stitch symbols into the inner lining of his traveling cloak. His needle traced neither elaborate vows nor Guild-sanctioned incantations, but instead formed a primitive mark—the kind of symbol that existed long before the Guild had claimed dominion over thread and memory.

A sigil that meant: *Protect. No matter what she becomes.*

The thread was ordinary cotton, nothing special about its material properties or magical resonance. But the intent he wove into its patterns transformed it into something more significant than its humble origins suggested—a visible reminder of the choice he'd made to bind his fate to hers regardless of what destinations that choice might ultimately demand.

As he worked, he thought about the vows he'd taken during his Guild training, the formal ceremonies that had made him an instrument of institutional will rather than an individual agent. Those oaths had been spoken aloud, witnessed by others, recorded in documents that became part of official history.

This commitment was different—private, personal, made without ceremony or witness. Not a vow to serve abstract principles, but a promise to protect someone specific, someone whose value couldn't be measured in terms of usefulness to larger causes.

She's afraid she's becoming a monster, he thought, pulling the final stitches tight and securing the thread with knots that would hold until the fabric itself wore away. *But monsters don't worry about the harm they might cause to others. Monsters don't cut their own palms to feel something they can control.*

Whatever forces sought to claim her, whatever prices would be demanded from both of them, he would stand between her and the darkness that whispered. Not because duty required it, but because love—the kind of protective devotion that transformed individuals into something more than the sum of their separate strengths—demanded nothing less.

The sigil complete, he stored the needle and thread away and settled back into his bedroll. He could rest in the knowledge that some battles were worth fighting regardless of their ultimate outcome.

Even if victory required becoming the kind of person he'd never thought he could be.

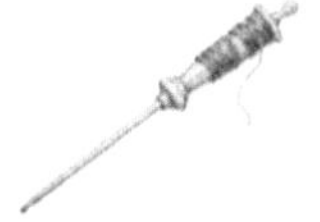

CHAPTER 5
Amara

The countryside between Eryndale and Feymont should have been peaceful. Rolling hills dotted with oak groves, meadows where wildflowers swayed in the afternoon breeze, streams that caught sunlight and threw it back in scattered diamonds. The kind of landscape that had inspired countless threadwork tapestries celebrating the simple beauty of seasons turning according to natural rhythm.

But something was wrong with the silence.

Amara paused beside a weathered waystone that marked an intersection of paths, her fingers tracing carvings that had been deliberately defaced. Where intricate patterns once guided travelers toward weaving shrines and market towns, crude scratches now obliterated their meaning with vandalism.

"They're erasing history," she said, studying damage that spoke of organized effort rather than random destruction. "Not just controlling the present, but making sure no one remembers what came before."

Caedric knelt beside the ruins of what had once been a small shrine, its altar stones scattered and blackened by fire that had burned hot enough to crack granite. The delicate threadwork that had once blessed travelers with protection and good fortune lay in charred fragments, reduced to ash that scattered in the wind.

"Standard purification protocols," he said, his voice carrying the clinical detachment of someone cataloging familiar techniques. "Remove all traces of unsanctioned practice, eliminate gathering points that might serve as rallying symbols. Make people forget they ever had alternatives to Guild oversight."

The explanation felt accurate but incomplete. This destruction went beyond practical considerations, crossing into something that resembled personal hatred for everything the old ways represented. As if the very existence of independent traditions posed a threat too fundamental to address through mere regulation.

Amara placed her palm flat against the largest piece of the broken altar, seeking some trace of the blessing that had once made this place sacred to traveling stitchers. The stone felt cold and dead, its spiritual resonance severed by those who had come to silence its song.

But as her hand lingered on the carved surface, she felt something stir. Not the gentle warmth she associated with her gift, but something deeper, darker, carrying frequencies that resonated with the bone runes that marked her flesh.

The tether pulse that shot through her palm felt like lightning made of shadow, connecting her to power sources she'd never learned to access. And in response to that unwanted contact, the altar began to change.

Threads of pale light emerged from cracks in the broken stone, weaving themselves into patterns that bridged the gaps created by deliberate destruction. Not healing the damage—the scars remained visible—but creating something new from the ruins, something that carried both the memory of what had been lost and the promise of what might yet be built.

"I didn't mean to do that," she whispered, pulling her hand away from stone that now hummed with restored purpose. The threads of light continued their work, creating a matrix of connection that extended beyond the immediate shrine, reaching toward other damaged sites with the patient persistence of roots seeking water.

Caedric watched the restoration with an expression she couldn't read—not fear, exactly, but something that might have been recognition of forces he'd hoped would remain dormant.

"Your gift is evolving," he said finally. "Growing beyond the boundaries you understood."

Evolution implied change that couldn't be reversed, adaptation that responded to environmental pressures rather than conscious choice. What she was becoming might be a natural response to the forces arrayed against her, but that didn't make the transformation any less terrifying.

How long before I can't control what I do? she wondered, studying the light-threads that continued weaving themselves through broken stone. *How long before the power decides what I should become?*

———◆———

The abandoned barn where they sheltered that night felt like a hollow ribcage, its weathered timbers rising into darkness that held the ghosts of seasons when it had served the living. Hay that should have fed livestock through winter months lay rotting in corners, while scythes and plowshares surrendered to rust, mute witnesses to villages scattered like seeds before the harvest could ever come.

Sleep came fitfully, interrupted by dreams that felt more vivid than waking experience. In them, she stood in a workshop filled with tools she'd never seen but somehow knew how to use. The Bone Spindle waited on a pedestal carved from a single piece of obsidian, its surface reflecting light that had nothing to do with normal fire.

Instead of merely observing, she reached for it.

The spindle felt warm in her hands, alive with potential that responded to her touch like an instrument that had been waiting for the right musician. Thread appeared at her fingertips—not cotton or wool or any material she recognized, but something that gleamed like captured starlight and felt as substantial as hope itself.

She began to spin, and with each turn of the spindle, reality bent to accommodate her intentions.

A wolf materialized from thread spun of hunger and moonlight, its eyes holding intelligence far beyond animal instinct. Not created, but summoned—called from a space where possibility waited to be given form.

A robe wove itself around her shoulders, its fabric stitched from prophecy made tangible, showing her visions of futures that might come to pass if she continued down the path she'd begun to walk. Some beautiful beyond description, others terrible enough to wake screaming from the most peaceful sleep.

And finally, inevitably, she found herself stitching Caedric's silhouette in threads that carried the essence of devotion made manifest. But as the work progressed, his form began to unravel, replaced by something else—someone else—whose features she couldn't quite discern through the haze of dream-logic.

Who are you replacing him with? part of her mind demanded. *What are you becoming that can't allow him to remain himself?*

But the dream-Amara continued her work with the methodical precision of someone following patterns written in her very bones, creating something from his dissolution that might serve purposes he'd never chosen to support.

She woke gasping, cold air shocking her lungs as consciousness pulled her back from visions that felt more like memory than imagination. Her fingertips burned with the phantom sensation of thread that had never existed, while wetness on her palms suggested she'd been bleeding in her sleep.

Looking down, she saw her hands covered with fine cuts, as if she'd been working with invisible needles, stitching patterns in the air above her chest. The wounds were shallow but numerous, creating a lacework of damage across her palms that spoke of hours spent in sleep-crafting she couldn't remember.

I was stitching, she realized with growing horror. *Actually stitching, not just dreaming about it.*

The recognition brought questions she wasn't ready to confront. If her dreams were becoming real, if the boundary between sleep and waking was dissolving under pressure from forces that sought to reshape her according to their own vision, how long before she lost the ability to distinguish between what she chose to do and what she was compelled to create?

The fire cast dancing shadows against the barn's walls as Amara sat beside Caedric, studying the cuts on her palms by flickering light that made every wound look deeper than it actually was. He'd offered salve for the injuries, but touching them felt important somehow—a reminder that some pain still belonged entirely to her.

The silence stretched between them, comfortable despite the weight of unspoken concerns. They'd developed a rhythm during their weeks on the road, an understanding of when words were needed and when presence was enough. But tonight felt different, charged with questions that had been building toward expression for longer than either wanted to acknowledge.

"Would you still follow me if I wasn't me anymore?" she asked, the words emerging without conscious decision to speak them.

He was quiet for so long that she began to think he wouldn't answer. When he finally spoke, his voice carried the careful weight of someone who'd considered the question from every possible angle.

"I'd follow you into fire," he said. "But I'd pull you back before you became it."

The response should have offered comfort, but instead it highlighted the central tension that had been growing between them. He was promising to protect her from herself, to serve as an anchor against currents that threatened to sweep her into strange waters beyond her mapping. But what if those forces proved stronger than individual will? What if the choice eventually came down to letting her burn or burning with her?

Their eyes met, and for a moment she saw past the professional restraint he maintained even in private moments. She saw concern that had deepened into something approaching devotion, loyalty that had evolved beyond duty into something more personal and therefore more dangerous.

He cares too much, she realized. *If I become what the tether wants me to become, it won't just destroy me. It'll destroy him too.*

The knowledge should have made her push him away, create distance that might protect him from whatever fate awaited her. But instead she found herself leaning slightly toward the warmth he represented—not just physical heat, but the emotional anchor of someone who'd chosen to stand with her despite every reason to walk away.

Fear won out over desire, as it always did. She broke their gaze, unable to bear what she saw there. Instead, she focused on the flames that devoured seasoned oak, crackling and spitting as they turned solid to smoke, obeying only the ancient, merciless alchemy that had ruled since the first spark fell on dry tinder.

———◆———

The farmer's wagon appeared around a bend in the forest path just after dawn, drawn by a placid mare whose steady pace suggested they'd been traveling since before sunrise. The old man who held the reins had the weathered hands and patient expression of someone who'd spent decades coaxing crops from reluctant soil, turning seed into sustenance through persistence and skill.

He offered them water from a leather flask without being asked, his eyes studying Amara with recognition that made her stomach clench with familiar unease. His gaze held not the shrewd measurement of a merchant, but the reverent gaze of a pilgrim who has finally glimpsed the shrine he'd begun to fear existed only in legend.

"You're her," he said simply. "The thread-witch. The one they're all talking about."

"I'm just someone trying to warn people about dangers they can't see," she replied, the words feeling increasingly hollow each time she spoke them. How could she claim to be ordinary when altars responded to her touch, when her dreams were beginning to reshape reality according to patterns she'd never consciously learned?

The farmer reached into his wagon and produced a small bundle wrapped in clean cloth, handling it with the reverence reserved for objects that carried spiritual significance beyond their material properties.

"From my daughter," he said, unwrapping a ribbon worked with the flame-and-loom sigil she'd seen in Eryndale. "She wanted me to give this to you if our paths crossed. Says the thread's moving, miss. Even if you don't see the stitching yet."

Amara accepted the gift with hands that trembled despite her attempts to project calm confidence. The ribbon was beautiful in its simplicity—common materials transformed into something meaningful through skill and intention. But it also represented something that terrified her more than Guild pursuit or the Weaver's whispered temptations.

They're making me into a symbol, she thought, studying threadwork that transformed her into an icon rather than an individual. *Turning my choices into their hope, my struggles into their inspiration.*

"How many people know that name?" she asked.

"Enough," the farmer replied. "Word travels fast when it carries the kind of hope people have been waiting for. Doesn't matter if you asked for it or not—some stories write themselves."

The conversation continued for a few more minutes, a careful exchange of information about road conditions and Guild patrols that might threaten travelers who couldn't afford official attention. But beneath the practical concerns lay something larger: the recognition that her mere existence had become a political statement, that her freedom represented possibility for communities that had forgotten they deserved alternatives to Guild oversight.

When the wagon disappeared around another bend, taking the farmer toward whatever destination called him, Amara found herself holding the ribbon like a physical weight of expectations she'd never asked to bear.

I want to help people make their own choices, she thought. *But they're choosing to follow me instead.*

———◆———

The smoke was visible from miles away—dark columns that rose straight up in the still air, carrying the distinctive odor of heirloom textiles and memory-thread dissolving in flames that could crack granite and melt the Guild's own runemarks. Not the thin wisps that rose from hearths or smithies, but thick plumes, the kind that left nothing but ash where generations of memory had once been preserved.

From the hilltop where they paused to study the valley below, Feymont looked like a wound carved into landscape that had once been beautiful. The weaving halls that had made the city famous throughout the region lay in ruins, their distinctive architecture reduced to blackened shells that would never again shelter the artisans who'd made the community culture possible.

Guild banners flew from improvised flagpoles, marking territory claimed through force rather than earned through service. But even at this distance, Amara could see that the occupation was temporary—the kind of thorough destruction that eliminated targets rather than controlling them.

"We're too late," she said, her voice carrying the flat tone of someone confronting failure that had been inevitable from the beginning.

Caedric studied the scene, counting patrol patterns and fortification positions. "The damage is recent. Maybe two days old. They're probably still in the area, making sure nothing recovers."

The tactical analysis was accurate, but it missed the larger tragedy. Feymont hadn't just been destroyed—it had been erased, transformed from a living community into a cautionary tale for anyone who might consider resistance to Guild authority. And they'd been too slow to prevent it, too focused on their own survival.

How many more cities will burn while we're still traveling between them? she wondered, watching smoke dissipate in the afternoon air. *How many communities will die because I couldn't move fast enough to save them?*

The ribbon in her pocket burned—not with magic, but with expectation. People she'd never met were embroidering her into their prayers, weaving her name into whispers of revolution. They saw a savior where she saw only a woman trying not to drown in powers she barely comprehended.

The thread's moving, the farmer had said. *Even if you don't see the stitching yet.*

But as she studied the ruins of what had once been a thriving community, Amara wondered if the pattern being woven was one of salvation or destruction. And whether, by the time she understood the difference, it would be too late to change the design.

The wind carried the scent of burned dreams across the valley, while Guild banners snapped in the breeze like prayers offered to gods of order and control. Somewhere ahead, other communities waited—unaware that their names were written on prophecy tapestries, unaware that their survival might depend on warnings from someone who wasn't sure she could trust herself to remain human long enough to deliver them.

But ready or not, the pattern was indeed moving. Whether by choice or by fate's design, she had become the single strand upon which the entire tapestry now depended.

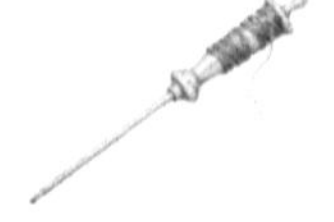

CHAPTER 6
Caedric

The merchant tunnel that led beneath Feymont's walls hadn't been used for legitimate trade in years, but it still served purposes that required discretion. Caedric remembered it from a Guild operation three winters past—not one of his missions, but close enough to the Hemlock Circle's activities that he'd studied the city's geography.

Now that same knowledge served a different role, guiding them through passages that smelled of old wine, bringing them up beneath a city that had been transformed into a cautionary tale for anyone who dared Guild authority.

They emerged through a concealed grate into an alley that should have echoed with the sounds of commerce and conversation. Instead, silence pressed against them, broken only by the distant crack of settling timbers as damaged buildings continued their slow collapse.

The devastation was thorough. Charred looms lay scattered in patterns that suggested they'd been dragged from workshops specifically to create public pyres. Thread-altars that had blessed the work of generations lay shattered.

Murals that had celebrated the city's weaving heritage were defaced with Hemlock sigils burned directly into stone, the Guild's mark of purity claiming ownership. The air carried the acrid smell of burned wool mixed with something else, something that made Caedric's trained senses recognize the distinctive odor of memories being erased.

They're not just controlling territory, he realized, studying the damage. *They're rewriting history, making it impossible for anyone to remember what came before.*

Amara moved through the destruction with an expression that had shifted beyond grief into something approaching numbness, and not the healthy numbness that protected minds from overwhelming trauma, but the dangerous kind that preceded a complete breakdown.

He watched her carefully, alert for signs that the tether might respond to emotional extremes by asserting stronger influence over her consciousness. The bone runes beneath her skin seemed more visible in the aftermath of destruction, as if exposure to the elimination of beauty and meaning fed the forces that sought to claim her for their own ends.

But for now, she remained herself—damaged but intact, horrified but still capable of choosing her responses to horror rather than being consumed by it.

The ambush came without warning as they moved deeper into the ruined city, three figures emerging from doorways with weapons. Not swords or Guild-issued equipment, but kitchen knives bound to broken loom shuttles, shards of pottery wrapped with cloth to serve as handles, tools of last resort wielded by people who'd been reduced to their final options.

"Stay back!" The voice belonged to a woman perhaps forty years old, her hair prematurely gray with stress, her hands shaking as she raised a makeshift spear toward Amara's chest. "We know what you are! We know why you're here!"

Guild informants, Caedric thought initially, his hand moving to the hilt of his thread-cutter. But something about their positioning felt wrong for trained agents— they moved like amateurs driven by terror rather than professionals executing planned operations.

Survivors, he realized. *People who escaped the purge and now assume anyone entering their city must represent additional threat.*

"Thread to thread, but never bone to bone," he said, speaking the recognition phrase that had once identified safe contacts among weavers. The effect was immediate. The three figures lowered their weapons—not completely, but enough to suggest they recognized the code as something other than immediate danger.

"How do you know the old words?" asked the woman with the spear, her voice carrying suspicion that hadn't entirely evaporated despite the recognition phrase. "Guild informants know them, too."

"Because I used to be Guild," Caedric replied, the admission feeling like stepping off a cliff into darkness. "And now I'm trying to help undo what I helped create."

For a moment that stretched into eternity, the woman studied his face with the careful attention of someone who'd learned that survival depended on accurate assessment of other people's motivations. Whatever she saw there—remorse, determination, the weight of choices that had reshaped his understanding of duty and honor—seemed to satisfy her immediate concerns.

"I'm Maela," she said, lowering the spear completely but keeping it within easy reach. "Former stitch-librarian of the Feymont Grand Hall. At least, I was until they decided our books contained seditious narratives."

Stitch-librarians were the keepers of community memory, responsible for preserving the techniques and stories that made weaving traditions immortal. If the Guild had targeted them specifically, it suggested their campaign of cultural erasure was even more comprehensive than the visible destruction indicated.

"They burned the libraries, too?" Amara asked, speaking for the first time since they'd entered the city.

Maela's expression darkened with grief that had settled into permanent features. "Everything. Techniques that had been preserved for centuries, pattern-books that held our ancestors' innovations, story-cycles that carried our community's history. All of it reduced to ash and smoke."

Cultural genocide, Caedric thought, studying the devastation with new understanding. *Not just controlling the present, but making sure no alternative versions of history survive to inspire future resistance.*

The recognition brought shame. He'd known the Guild's methods, had participated in operations that eliminated "problematic elements" from target populations. But he'd told himself those actions served the greater good, protected innocent people from corruption that might otherwise spread beyond control.

Now, seeing the results through the eyes of someone who'd chosen different loyalties, he understood what those operations actually accomplished. Not protection, but erasure. Not order, but the kind of sterile uniformity that eliminated everything beautiful or meaningful in favor of compliance that asked no questions about what it was complying with.

━━◆━━

The hidden sanctuary lay beneath a collapsed dye house. The cellar held perhaps thirty people. Children whose eyes held the hollow look of trauma that had stolen their voices, and adults who moved with the carefulness of those who'd learned that any gesture might be interpreted as threatening. Their hands were bound with soft cloth. Not restraints, but self-imposed limitations designed to prevent "accidental" stitching that might alert Guild truth-readers to their location.

They're so afraid of their own gifts that they've crippled themselves, Caedric observed, watching people who should have been creating beauty instead hiding from their own nature. *This is what the Guild's version of order actually produces—not compliance, but the kind of fear that turns capabilities into curses.*

Amara knelt beside a group of children who huddled together near the chamber's warmest corner, not speaking but simply offering her presence as acknowledgment that their suffering mattered to someone. The gesture was small, but Caedric watched the way their expressions shifted in response—not a dramatic transformation, but the subtle easing that came when people who'd been forgotten remembered what it felt like to be seen.

And he noticed something else: the way the adults looked at her. Not just with fear, though that was present, but with something approaching hope. As if her mere existence proved that survival was possible, that resistance didn't necessarily end in death or disappearance.

She's becoming what they need her to be, he realized. *Whether she wants it or not, whether she's ready for it or not, they're making her into the symbol they can rally behind.*

That evening, when the day's tension had settled into exhausted quiet, Caedric found himself in conversation with the sanctuary's elders. It wasn't a formal meeting—those required resources and optimism these people couldn't afford—but the kind of careful discussion that explored possibilities without committing to actions that might prove fatal.

"The Guild is afraid," he said, keeping his voice low enough that it wouldn't carry to the children who finally slept in corners of the chamber. "Their recent escalation, this destruction—these aren't the tactics of an organization that feels secure in its authority."

Maela studied him. "What do you mean?"

"Fear makes institutions cruel, but it also makes them sloppy. They're overreacting to threats they can't properly identify, using excessive force because they've lost confidence in their ability to maintain control through subtler methods."

The analysis was accurate as far as it went, but incomplete. What he didn't say—couldn't say without revealing knowledge that might endanger everyone present—was that his former colleagues in the Hemlock Circle had been showing signs of the same fear for months before he'd abandoned his post to protect Amara.

Whispered conversations about "containment failures" and "expanding corruption networks." Emergency protocols that had been activated without public acknowledgment. The kind of systematic paranoia that suggested the Guild's leadership was responding to threats larger than any individual practitioner represented.

They know something is coming, he thought. *Something they can't control through their usual methods.*

"What are you suggesting?" asked another elder.

"Help us reopen one of the old message looms," Caedric said. "Broadcast a call that looks like innocent pattern-sharing but actually carries coded instructions for a coordinated resistance."

He wasn't just asking them to risk their lives—they were already doing that by merely surviving—but to risk hope, which for people who'd lost everything was a far more precious commodity.

"Why?" Maela's question was simple, but it cut to the heart of motivations that Caedric was still learning to understand. "Why help us? Why care now?"

He could have offered justifications, strategic explanations about weakening Guild authority or creating diversionary actions that might protect other targets. All of which would have been true as far as they went.

Instead, he chose honesty that felt like stepping naked into winter wind.

"Because I know what I helped build," he said, his gaze moving briefly to Amara where she sat beside the sleeping children. "And I know who I want to help tear it down."

The acknowledgment wasn't merely that he had once supported systems he now rejected, but that personal motivations had turned distant ideals into urgent commitments. Not a duty to grand causes, but devotion to a single person whose worth had nothing to do with usefulness.

The gift came the next morning as they prepared to leave the sanctuary, delivered by a child perhaps eight years old who approached Amara with careful ceremony. In her small hands she carried a piece of cloth that had been worked with threads salvaged from the destruction above—not a formal tapestry, but a simple image that showed remarkable skill despite its humble materials.

Amara's face, rendered in stitches that captured not just physical features but something of the expression she wore when she thought no one was watching—hope and fear and determination woven together in patterns that spoke of artistic vision.

Below the portrait, worked in letters that combined traditional threadwork with symbols that were purely the child's invention, was a single word: *Threadmarked.*

"For you," the girl said, offering the cloth with reverence. "So you remember us when you're far away."

Amara stared at the image of herself, her expression shifting through emotions too complex for easy categorization. Wonder at the skill that had created beauty from materials salvaged from destruction. Horror at seeing herself transformed into an icon rather than an individual. Guilt at accepting hope from people who'd already sacrificed more than anyone should be asked to bear.

She started to hand it back, overwhelmed by implications she couldn't fully process. But Caedric caught her wrist, his fingers gentle but firm as they prevented the gesture.

"They need this," he said quietly. "Even if you don't."

For a moment, their eyes met across the space that had grown between them—not physical distance, but the emotional gap created by fears neither of them knew how to voice. Without speaking, she folded the cloth carefully and placed it in her satchel. The gesture was small, but everyone in the chamber seemed to sense its significance— the moment when someone stepped across the line between individual and symbol, between person and cause.

Threadmarked, Caedric thought, watching the child's face light up with joy at having her gift accepted. Not thread-witch, with its implications of supernatural power divorced from human concerns, but something that acknowledged both her magical abilities and her connection to the communities that looked to her for inspiration.

She's not just fighting the Guild anymore, he understood. *She's becoming the focal point for everyone who refuses to accept that the Guild's version of order is the only possibility.*

The recognition should have terrified him—revolutions were dangerous things, as likely to consume their own supporters as their intended enemies. Instead, it felt like vindication of choices that had seemed impossible when he'd first made them.

Whatever came next, whatever prices would be demanded from all of them, he'd helped create something that hadn't existed before: hope that resistance was possible, proof that the Guild's authority could be challenged by people who refused to accept that survival required the surrender of everything that made survival meaningful.

For the first time since he'd abandoned his Guild commission to protect her, Caedric began to believe they might actually succeed in building something better from the ruins of what they were learning to destroy.

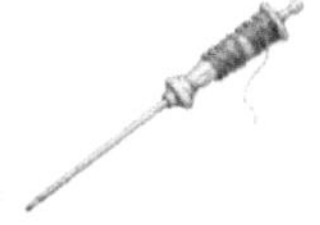

CHAPTER 7
Amara

The Tapestrum Loom waited beneath layers of dust and mourning cloth like a sleeping giant, its massive frame carved from heartwood. As Maela led them down into the sanctuary's deepest chamber, Amara felt something stir in response to the ancient weaving apparatus—not her usual gift, but something deeper, darker, that resonated with the bone runes beneath her skin.

"The weavers built it during the first Guild Wars," Maela explained. "When communication between cities became impossible through normal channels, this let them send patterns across distances. Codes with warnings and hope."

The loom's threads stretched taut between posts that rose toward the chamber's ceiling, their surfaces gleaming with residual enchantment that had never entirely faded despite years of disuse. Not ordinary fiber, but something that existed in the space between material and spirit, capable of carrying meaning across distances that physical matter couldn't bridge.

Pattern-casting, Amara recognized, remembering fragments of a story her grandmother had told her. The ability to weave messages directly into the fabric of reality, sending information through channels that transcended normal limitations of space and time.

"It's dangerous," Caedric said, studying the loom's construction with wariness. "Broadcasts like this are traceable. If the Guild still monitors the old channels, using it will announce our location to every truth-reader in the region."

"More dangerous than letting people face the Guild without warning?" Maela countered. "More dangerous than letting communities be destroyed one by one because they don't know what's coming?"

Amara found herself caught between loyalties. To Caedric, whose concern for her safety had become the foundation of choices that shaped both their lives, and to people who needed hope more than they needed protection.

If I don't speak now, then when? she thought, studying the loom that offered the possibility of reaching communities too distant for personal warning. *When they're already burning? When it's too late for anyone to choose their own response?*

The decision crystallized as she remembered the ribbon in her satchel— simple cloth worked with the flame-and-loom. The farmer who'd given it to her had spoken of threads moving, patterns being woven by forces larger than any single person could control.

But patterns required weavers. And if people were looking to her to provide direction, if her name was being whispered in coded conversations and resistance cells, then perhaps it was time to stop hiding from the role that circumstances had thrust upon her.

I'm not ready to be a leader, she acknowledged, approaching the loom with hands that trembled despite her efforts to project confidence. *But maybe no one ever is. Maybe leadership is something you grow into by accepting the responsibility rather than waiting until you feel capable of bearing it.*

The ancient threads responded to her touch, their surfaces warming beneath her fingers as dormant enchantments recognized the presence of someone with the gift to activate their hidden purposes. Not forcing compliance, but offering partnership—the difference between commanding tools and collaborating with them.

I can do this, she told herself, settling into the seat that had been carved to accommodate the loom's operator. *I can weave a message that reaches beyond Feymont, that gives people the chance to choose their own responses to what's coming.*

But even as she formed the thought, she felt something else stirring. The tether that bound her to the Weaver of Bone pulsed with interest, responding to the large-scale magical working. Not commanding her actions, but observing with satisfaction as she reached for power that normal threadwork couldn't provide.

You are learning, whispered the Weaver's voice. *Learning to embrace what you were made to become.*

She pushed the whisper aside, focusing instead on the pattern she needed to weave. Not the dark visions that haunted her dreams, but something that carried hope rather than corruption. The message took shape beneath her hands with surprising clarity, as if the words had been waiting for expression longer than she'd realized. Not complex poetry or elaborate metaphor, but simple communication that could be decoded by anyone with basic knowledge of traditional pattern-work.

To the hidden looms, the silent shuttles, the hands that remember what hearts have not forgotten:

The Guild burns what they cannot control, but fire creates ash, and ash nurtures new growth. The Threadmarked rises. The Pattern frays. Gather your courage and rejoin the weave.

Southern paths lead to Rilan's Hollow, where the old agreements wait to be renewed.

Bring your gifts, your stories, your refusal to surrender.

Thread to thread, but never bone to bone. The design is not yet finished.

Each word materialized in the loom's pattern as threads that gleamed with inner light, carrying meaning that transcended the symbols through which it was expressed. Not just information, but intent—the kind of purposeful communication that could bridge distances between minds as well as bodies.

As she worked, Amara felt the tether's influence growing stronger, feeding on the magical energy that flowed through the pattern-casting. The bone runes beneath her skin began to pulse in rhythm with the loom's ancient heartbeat, creating harmony between her personal corruption and the tool's designed purpose.

This is what you could accomplish if you stopped limiting yourself, the Weaver's voice observed with satisfaction that made her stomach clench. *This is merely the beginning of what we could create together.*

But she held steady, focusing on the faces of the people who'd trusted her with their hopes rather than the whispers that sought to transform that hope into something darker. The children who slept in the sanctuary above, the adults who'd bound their own hands rather than risk detection, the communities that waited unaware for warnings that might save their lives.

I'm not doing this for power, she reminded herself, pulling the final threads tight to seal the pattern's intent. *I'm doing this because no one should be forced into silence or obedience.*

The moment the last knot was tied, the loom exploded into activity. Light raced along its ancient threads like wildfire through dry grass, carrying the encoded message toward destinations that she'd never seen. Not traveling through physical space, but threading through hidden connections.

The sanctuary's survivors watched in reverent silence as magic they'd only heard described in stories materialized before their eyes. Light-threads spiraled upward through stone and earth, seeking the hidden channels that would carry warnings to faraway places.

It's beautiful, Amara thought, watching her message disappear into the web. *This is what threadwork was meant to accomplish.*

But even as she admired the ancient loom's purpose, she again felt the tether that bound her to the Weaver pulse with satisfaction, as if her use of the pattern-casting had strengthened what she'd been trying to weaken.

"You lit a signal fire," Caedric said, moving to examine the loom for signs of dangerous resonance. His face was creased with concern that shifted toward alarm. "They might see it."

A trace pulse lingers, she realized, sensing echoes of her message that continued to reverberate through the loom's enchanted framework. Not the intended broadcast, but something else—a magical signature that could be tracked back to its source by anyone with the proper training.

"Good," she said, the word emerging with conviction that surprised her. "Let them see it. Let them know that people refuse to be eliminated quietly."

The response from those present was immediate. Three of the sanctuary's survivors stepped forward.

"We want to join you," said a young man. "We'll meet you in Rilan's Hollow to help with whatever you're building there."

Others remained in the shadows, their expressions revealing internal struggles between hope and fear, between the desire to act and the instinct for survival that had kept them alive through systematic persecution. But even those who didn't volunteer watched with interest that suggested seeds had been planted, possibilities considered that hadn't existed before her message went out.

The movement is starting, Amara understood, studying faces that reflected cautious optimism. The recognition should have pleased her, but instead it felt like weight settling around her shoulders. Leadership carried responsibilities she'd never asked to bear, obligations to people who looked to her for answers she didn't possess and guidance she wasn't qualified to provide.

I'm not the hero they want, she thought. *I'm just someone who refused to accept that the*

Guild's version of order was the only possibility. But maybe that's enough. Maybe I don't need to be perfect—I just need to be willing to try building something better from the ruins of what we're destroying.

The Guild will respond, she knew. *They'll send everything they have to stop what we're building before it grows large enough to threaten their control.*

Amara walked through the ruins of Feymont, followed by those who'd chosen hope over safety. The Pattern was indeed fraying, but perhaps that was necessary. Perhaps some designs needed to be unraveled before better ones could take their place.

And perhaps she was exactly the weaver they needed to guide them.

CHAPTER 8
Caedric

The countryside between Feymont and their destination stretched out in rolling waves of gold-touched grass that caught the dying light like scattered coins. For the first time in weeks, the horizon held no smoke columns and no Guild banners. Just fields where wildflowers nodded in the evening breeze, a small herd of deer that startled at their approach before bounding away through tall grass, and the kind of peaceful silence that only nature offered.

Caedric walked beside Amara through the temporary sanctuary, his eyes moving between the path ahead and her profile where the wind played through her dark hair that had grown longer during their flight. Dirt streaked her cheeks from the morning's climb through rocky terrain, while exhaustion had carved subtle lines around her eyes, eyes that held depths he was still learning to navigate.

She's beautiful, he thought, the recognition hitting him with a force that had nothing to do with physical attraction and everything to do with the way she carried herself despite the weight of burdens she'd never asked to bear. *Even worn thin.*

The observation should have been casual, the kind of aesthetic appreciation that required no further consideration. Instead, it felt like an acknowledgment of his feelings. *I've faced traitors, monsters, and worse,* he realized, watching her pause to study a cluster of flowers. *But this? This is what terrifies me most.*

Not the Guild pursuit that followed wherever they went, though that carried genuine danger. Not the tether that bound her to the Weaver of Bone, though that threatened corruption worse than death. But the growing certainty that what he felt for her had moved into territory he'd never learned to navigate.

Tonight, he decided. *I'll tell her tonight.*

They made camp beside a stream that sang over stones worn smooth by countless seasons, its voice providing counterpoint to the evening sounds of insects and night birds. The fire he built was small, barely large enough to cook their simple meal, but sufficient to create an intimate space.

Amara sat across the flames from him, tending to her boots. The leather was worn thin in places, patched with strips of cloth that spoke of resourcefulness born from necessity rather than choice.

"I never expected rebellion to require so much walking," she said, her tone carrying humor that had become more precious because it appeared so rarely. "All the stories focus on dramatic confrontations and stirring speeches. None of them mention blisters."

The observation drew a smile from him— genuine amusement that felt like an unexpected gift in circumstances that offered few reasons for lightness. "The stories leave out most of the practical details. They don't mention that heroes spend more time hungry and tired than they do inspiring others to greatness."

"Good thing we're not heroes then," she replied, but her expression had shifted toward something more serious. "Just people trying to make choices that might matter to someone other than ourselves."

Heroes existed in stories as simplified ideals, not in the lived reality of survival, where choices were tangled, consequences unavoidable, and no path remained clear.

Heroes belonged to stories, abstractions that existed to serve narrative purposes rather than navigate the complicated realities of individual survival in circumstances that offered no clean solutions. But normal people were real and present, capable of choices that rose above the roles others tried to impose upon them.

Like the choice I'm about to make, he thought, studying her face across the fire that painted her features in shades of gold and shadow. *Like the words I've been carrying for weeks without finding the courage to speak them.*

"There's something I need to say," he began, the words emerging with difficulty. Not because they were hard to form, but because honesty demanded a vulnerability he wasn't used to. "Something I should have said before Feymont..."

Amara looked up from her boots, curiosity flickering in her expression as she recognized the weight his voice carried.

"Caedric?" she prompted when the silence stretched longer than was comfortable.

He opened his mouth to continue, to speak the words that would transform the careful professional distance they'd maintained into something more personal and therefore more dangerous...

Amara suddenly doubled over as if struck by an invisible force, her hands flying to her temples while a cry escaped her lips. Not the sharp sound of physical injury, but something deeper—the distorted expression of consciousness that had been pushed aside by something else entirely.

"Amara!" Caedric was beside her in an instant, his incomplete confession forgotten as his instincts reasserted themselves. But this wasn't a situation that Guild training had prepared him to address, wasn't the kind of threat that could be countered through tactical knowledge or superior force.

Her eyes had gone pale white, pupils disappearing into irises that reflected light like polished bone. Threads from her traveling pack began to unravel without being touched, rising into the air around her body to weave patterns that had nothing to do with her conscious will.

When she spoke again, her voice carried layers that belonged to someone else entirely.

"She must open the pattern further. Push her forward, or I will."

The words emerged from her throat, but they weren't hers. Caedric recognized the cadences despite having hoped never to hear them again—the Weaver of Bone, speaking through the tether that bound him to Amara's consciousness.

He hasn't possessed her, he realized. *He's using her as a conduit for a message.*

"Amara," he called, gripping her shoulders with hands that trembled despite his efforts to remain calm. "Can you hear me? You need to come back."

Her hands moved in the air above her chest, tracing patterns that glowed faintly in the firelight while her lips whispered words in languages he didn't know or understand.

She's disappearing, he understood with clarity that cut through his panic. *Whatever the tether is doing to her, she's losing the battle to remain herself.*

Flashes of memory began to project through the threadlight that surrounded her—not his memories, but hers, offered like glimpses through windows into experiences that had shaped her into the person he'd chosen to protect.

Her grandmother's weathered hands teaching basic stitching techniques while firelight painted the walls in golden warmth. The first time she'd brought dead fabric back to life, wonder and terror warring in her young face as she'd realized she had the gift. Her palm pressed against his as they'd worked together at the Feymont loom.

She's trying to show me something, he realized, studying the projected memories for patterns that might reveal how to reach her.

Trying to find her way back through experiences that belong entirely to her.

Without thinking, he raised his hand and struck her cheek—not hard enough to cause injury, but sharp enough to shock, hoping physical sensation might serve as an anchor to pull her back from the internal battlefield she was fighting.

"Come back to me, Amara," he said, speaking to the memories that might still carry traces of the person he'd grown to care for more than duty or doctrine. "You're stronger than him. You're stronger than anything he can threaten you with."

For a moment that stretched into eternity, nothing changed. The threadlight continued its alien patterns, her voice continued whispering in foreign languages, her eyes continued to reflect light that had nothing to do with the campfire.

Then she gasped—a sharp intake of breath that spoke of consciousness returning from places it had never been meant to go—and collapsed forward into his arms.

Caedric caught her as she fell, wrapping his cloak around her shoulders. She shook with exhaustion that went far beyond physical fatigue, and her breathing was shallow but steady. Her pulse raced, and her face was pale, but it was recognizably her own rather than a mask worn by someone else.

She came back, he thought, holding her against his chest while relief washed over him in waves that left him trembling almost as badly as she was. *Whatever the Weaver tried to do to her, she found her way back to herself.*

But the victory felt temporary, fragile as morning frost that would disappear the moment circumstances changed. The tether that bound her to him was growing stronger rather than weaker, feeding on the magical exertion that her expanding role required.

How many more times can she fight this battle? he wondered, studying her unconscious face for signs of damage the intrusion might have caused. *How long before the choice is no longer hers to make?*

The woods around their small camp seemed darker now, filled with shadows that might hide threats he couldn't identify or combat through conventional means. Guild pursuit was dangerous but comprehensible.

Soldiers followed predictable patterns, responded to tactical considerations, could be outmaneuvered through superior knowledge of terrain and timing.

But this was something else entirely. A war being fought on a battlefield that existed in the space between consciousness and dream, individual will and external compulsion. Territory he had no training to navigate, equipped with weapons that might prove useless against enemies that existed primarily as concepts rather than physical opponents.

The confession he'd been preparing felt distant now, overwhelmed by recognition of how close he'd come to losing her—not to death, which would have grieved him, but to the transformation into something that merely wore her face.

But the words needed to be spoken anyway, even if she couldn't hear them. Even if they changed nothing about the forces arrayed against them or the prices that would be demanded from both of them.

"I love you," he whispered to the wind that carried his words toward horizons they might never reach together. "And I'm not letting him have you."

CHAPTER 9
Amara

She opened her eyes to a sky that was alien.

Not the familiar blue of day or the star-scattered black of night, but something that looked like an ancient tapestry coming apart at the seams. Threads of light and shadow wove through the clouds, while patches of darkness gaped like holes torn in fabric.

Below the impossible sky lay the city where she'd grown up: stone cottages with thatched roofs, narrow lanes that wound between herb gardens and workshop yards, the old basement room where her grandmother had taught her the basic techniques that had shaped her understanding of weaving.

But everything was wrong here, too.

The buildings were stitched together with filaments that gleamed like polished bone, their surfaces pulsing with light. Windows showed not the warm glow of hearth flames but the radiance of materials that belonged neither fully to life or death.

This isn't real, she understood with the dream logic that accepted impossibility while recognizing its fundamental nature. *This is the tether. This is what he wants me to see.*

Looking down at her hands, she found them marked with sigils that glowed beneath her skin—not the bone runes that had begun appearing in waking life, but something more complete. Weaving symbols she'd never learned, pattern-codes that carried meaning she couldn't decipher.

The bone mirror, knowledge whispered from a source she didn't recognize. *Where possibility shows its face to those brave enough to look.*

The streets filled with figures as she walked—not people exactly, but shapes that wore human form. Faceless weavers who moved with the mechanical movements of tools rather than the organic uncertainty of living beings.

They chanted as she passed, their voices harmonizing in ways that normal throats couldn't achieve.

"Threadmarked. Boneborn. The Pattern made flesh."

One by one, they knelt as she approached, offering reverence that felt like worship stripped of everything voluntary or joyful. Not the hopeful recognition she'd seen in Feymont's survivors, but the kind of absolute submission that left no room for individual choice or disagreement.

This is what power looks like, she realized with growing horror. *The elimination of free will.*

A child emerged from the crowd—or something that wore a child's shape. In her small hands she held a garment that might once have been beautiful, but was now soaked with stains that looked disturbingly like dried blood.

"Thank you," the child-thing said, offering the ruined cloth with the same reverence the others had shown. "You stitched my father into obedience. Now he only speaks the words you've chosen for him."

This was what she could accomplish if she stopped limiting herself to gentle influence, if she embraced techniques that worked directly on the threads that bound consciousness to individual will.

Complete control, the tether whispered through her awareness. *No more resistance, no more suffering caused by people making choices that harm themselves and others. Just the peace that comes when everything serves its proper purpose.*

At the village's center, where the old market square had once hosted gatherings that celebrated community through voluntary participation, a throne waited.

Not carved from stone or wood, but woven from ivory needles that gleamed with their own inner light. Around it, looms operated without human touch, their shuttles moving according to the will of unseen hands. Threads crawled across the ground like living things, seeking materials they could incorporate into the vast tapestry that seemed to encompass the entire impossible landscape.

This is what I could become, she understood, studying the seat of power that had been prepared for her acceptance. *Not a servant to forces beyond my understanding, but their willing partner in reshaping the world.*

Her reflection in a basin of dark water showed her clad in a gown woven from sinew and power, her eyes as pale as a winter sky, her hands moving in patterns that rewrote reality with each gesture. Beautiful, in its way. Perfect, according to standards that measured value in terms of efficiency rather than choice.

The Guild fears you because they see a threat to their authority, the tether observed. *But I see potential that goes far beyond mere opposition to their particular vision of order.*

The Weaver of Bone materialized beside the throne—not the monstrous figure she'd encountered, but something elegant and terrible. Tall and graceful, wearing an ageless beauty that came from having transcended the limitations that bound normal existence to cycles of growth and decay.

This is what he really looks like, she realized. *Not corruption, but perfection that has moved beyond the need for human concerns like consent or mercy.*

"Every stitch you pull tight binds you to me," he said, his voice carrying harmonies that resonated with the bone runes beneath her skin. "Every act of defiance, every miracle you perform in service of your chosen causes—all of it draws you closer to accepting what you were made to become."

His gesture encompassed the whole of it: the surrounding landscape, the throne poised for her claim, and the faceless weavers who were subsumed by something greater than individuality.

"The Guild sees you as a threat because they recognize that your power challenges their authority. But they understand so little of what you actually represent. You're not their enemy—you're their replacement. The next stage in the evolution of control, refined beyond their crude methods into something truly transcendent."

The words carried a truth that existed independent of whether she wanted to accept it. Every time she'd used her gift to accomplish what normal techniques couldn't achieve, every moment she'd pushed beyond the boundaries that had once defined her understanding of possible, she'd taken steps down a path that led toward the throne that gleamed with bonelight.

We are inevitable, the truth whispered through her consciousness. *Not because I compel your choices, but because the logic of power leads only in one direction. You can preserve what you value only by claiming the authority to eliminate what threatens it.*

For a moment that felt timeless, she was tempted.

The idea of control—real control, sufficient to end the Guild's systematic oppression, to eliminate the Wraithstitchers who tortured innocent people for their own purposes, to create a world where no one had to run or hide or sacrifice their humanity for the sake of mere survival—it called to her with pull that felt like gravity itself.

No more choosing between bad options and worse ones. No more watching communities burn because I couldn't reach them in time. No more accepting that some forms of suffering are inevitable.

But as she reached toward the throne, she caught sight of something that didn't belong in this perfected landscape. A piece of cloth, torn and mended with careful stitches that spoke of love. Caedric's traveling cloak.

His voice calling her back from the darkness that sought to claim her consciousness. The weight of his hands on her shoulders as he'd fought to reach her through forces that had tried to displace her awareness. The promise in his touch that some bonds couldn't be severed by corruption or compulsion.

Memory flooded through her—not the perfected visions that the tether offered, but the messy reality of choices made by people who refused to accept that survival came at the cost of what made it matter.

The child in Feymont who'd given her the portrait worked in salvaged threads. The survivors who'd chosen to follow her despite every reason to prioritize their own safety. The farmer who'd offered hope that traveled faster than any Guild courier.

Her grandmother's warning, spoken over tea and firelight years before the Guild had taken an interest in her family's gifts: "Don't look too long into the darkness, child. It has a way of convincing you that its vision of light is the only one worth seeking."

"I'd rather be unraveled than become you," she said, her voice carrying conviction that surprised her with its strength.

She threw down the bone-threaded cloak that had materialized in her hands, rejecting the gift that would have completed her transformation. The throne cracked. The faceless weavers began to dissolve. The impossible sky started tearing itself apart with sounds like fabric ripping under impossible tension.

"You will return," the Weaver's voice followed her as the vision collapsed around them both. *"When the choices become impossible, when the prices become too high, when the people you're trying to protect demand what you cannot provide—you will remember what I offered."*

Consciousness returned, shocking her back into awareness of her physical body sprawled in Caedric's arms beside the dying embers of their campfire. Dawn light filtered through trees that remained stubbornly real, while bird songs joined the sound of stream water.

Her body was soaked with sweat, while phantom sensations of thread moving beneath her skin reminded her that the vision's effects weren't entirely confined to dream. Sigils still glowed faintly across her fingers—not the complete transformations she'd seen in the bone mirror, but evidence that the tether's influence was growing stronger rather than weaker.

It wasn't just showing me possibility, she realized, her thoughts still foggy from the lingering disorientation. *It was trying to make that possibility inevitable.*

"Amara." Caedric's voice carried relief mixed with concern. "You're back. You're safe."

Safe, she thought, studying hands that still tingled with residual power. *Am I? Can anyone be safe?*

But his arms around her felt real in ways that complicated the questions about what constituted genuine versus artificial experience. Anchor points in reality that couldn't be dissolved by the forces that sought to convince her that individual choice was an illusion.

"The tether," she said, her voice barely above a whisper. "It's not just connected to him anymore. It's... growing. Becoming part of me in ways I can't control."

She wanted to tell him about the throne that had waited for her acceptance, but the words wouldn't come—not because the tether prevented their expression, but because some truths were too dangerous to speak aloud, even to people who'd earned the right to hear them.

What if he sees the temptation in my eyes? What if he understands that part of me wanted to accept what was offered?

Instead, she pressed closer to his warmth, choosing connection to humanity over the isolation that power promised. Not because the choice was easy, but because some things deserved to endure, even at the cost of accepting imperfect outcomes.

"Whatever thread binds you to him," Caedric said, "we'll cut it. Together."

Even as she accepted the comfort his words offered, she wondered if cutting the tether would prove possible—or if the connection had already grown beyond the point where separation could be achieved without destroying everything it had grown to encompass.

Including me, she thought, studying the sigils that continued to fade from her fingers. *Including the person I've been before this started, and everyone who depends on that person making choices they can live with.*

The bone mirror had shown her what she could become if she stopped fighting, but it had also reminded her why that change came at prices too high for any individual to pay while remaining human.

Whatever came next, she would hold to the memory of torn cloth mended with love, to the voice that called her back from darkness.

CHAPTER 10
Caedric

Vel Oris spread below them like a corpse dressed for burial—too still, too clean. From their hidden position on the ridge overlooking the city, Caedric studied the streets that should have been clogged with merchant wagons and textile traders, but instead patrols of Guild enforcers moved between checkpoints.

"They knew we were coming," he said, lowering the spyglass that confirmed what his instincts had already recognized. "The map isn't just a prophecy. It's bait."

Amara crouched beside him among the scrub brush that provided concealment from eyes below, her expression scrunching with recognition of the trap. It wasn't random Guild presence, but a focused deployment that spoke of specific intelligence about their movements and destinations.

"The Tapestrum broadcast," she said, the words carrying a hint of guilt. "They must have intercepted part of the message, traced it back to discover our route."

The conclusion was logical, but it missed crucial considerations that Caedric's Guild training had taught him to recognize. Surveillance at this level required more than intercepted communications. It demanded coordinated intelligence gathering across multiple cities, resources that suggested a commitment far beyond normal enforcement protocols.

They're not just hunting us anymore, he realized, studying banners that flew from improvised flagpoles throughout the occupied city. *They're preparing for war.*

Hemlock Circle standards marked checkpoints that controlled every route into Vel Oris, while truth-readers examined each traveler coming into the city. This wasn't a general security measure, but a targeted operation.

Caedric also noticed the specialized units, forces called in only when ordinary enforcement failed, and when a problem needed to be eradicated rather than contained.

That night they made camp in a grove of standing stones, ancient markers where agreements between communities had been sealed with blood and thread long before institutional oversight decided that such arrangements required official sanction. No fire, no cooked food, nothing that might reveal their position to watchers who could be anywhere in the darkness that surrounded their temporary refuge.

Caedric positioned himself where he could observe anyone directly approaching while Amara rested against one of the carved monoliths, though sleep seemed unlikely given the tension that radiated from her like heat from forge coals. Every shadow might hide enemies, every sound could herald discovery, every moment brought them closer to confrontation.

She's afraid to use her gift, he observed, watching her hands tremble as she fought the urge to trace protective patterns in the air above her chest. The bone mirror vision had shaken her more than physical injury could have, leaving her uncertain.

The air grew still. Not the comfortable quiet of evening settling into night, but something deliberate, artificial, imposed by an unnatural force. Threads on his traveling cloak began to tremble despite the absence of any breeze, while a single strand danced against gravity with movements that spoke of manipulation by unseen hands.

We're not alone.

"Amara," he said, drawing his thread-cutter soundlessly. "Wake up. Quietly."

Her eyes opened immediately, pupils dilated. No questions about his assessment, no demands for explanation—just instant readiness for whatever danger he had identified.

The figure emerged from the shadows, their approach so silent that only supernatural alertness had provided warning of their presence. Pitch-black garments absorbed light rather than reflecting it, making them difficult to track even when direct observation should have made concealment impossible.

Their face was hidden behind a mask stitched from materials that seemed to shift and flow despite remaining fundamentally unchanged, while each movement carried the fluid grace of someone who'd been trained to kill without leaving evidence that murder had occurred. They didn't wear a Guild uniform, but something more specialized—equipment designed for operations that required complete deniability.

Thread Assassin, Caedric confirmed, recognizing the techniques that had been whispered about in Hemlock Circle briefings but never officially acknowledged. Elite operatives who existed only in the most classified documents.

"They don't arrest," he said, raising his blade into a defensive position while stepping between Amara and the approaching figure. "They erase."

The assassin attacked without warning, hands moving in patterns that produced weapons from the very air around them. Thread-woven garrotes materialized between their fingers, while silken darts emerged from sleeves designed to conceal an arsenal of weapons that existed primarily as potential until called into being.

The fight was unlike anything Caedric had known in his years with the Guild. This wasn't the clean clash of sword on sword, but a lethal exchange where steel met powers that bent reality itself to the will of the one wielding them.

The assassin moved like liquid, flowing between attack and defense with transitions so smooth they seemed to exist outside the normal limitations of physics. Garrotes became binding nets, darts transformed into seeking threads that pursued their targets despite evasive maneuvers, while the very air seemed to thicken in response to gestures that rewrote the rules governing physical interaction.

Caedric parried strikes that came from angles that shouldn't have been possible while seeking openings in the assassin's defenses that shifted faster than he could exploit. Behind him, he could sense Amara.

Her gift stirred in response to the magical combat that surrounded them.

She's afraid of becoming what the vision showed her, he understood, dodging a garrote that would have opened his throat if his reflexes had been a fraction slower. *Afraid that using her power will pull her closer to accepting what the Weaver offers.*

The assassin's next attack came with killing intent that left no room for defensive maneuvering—a combination of thread-weapons that forced him to choose between protecting himself and shielding Amara from strikes that could prove instantly fatal.

Without conscious decision, he threw himself into the path of silken darts that dissolved on impact, their magical toxins flooding his system with numbness that spread from the point of contact outward.

I'm not going to be able to stop him soon, he realized, feeling the strength drain from limbs that were losing their ability to respond to conscious direction. I *need to end this now, before the poison reaches my heart.*

Desperation bred innovation. Instead of fighting against the assassin's thread-weapons, he grabbed the next garrote that came within reach and used his knowledge to reverse its magical properties. Not dispelling the enchantment, but turning it back on its creator with force amplified by their own power.

The thread-weapon became a trap that the assassin couldn't escape, binding them in coils of their own making while the magic they'd woven to kill others instead served to incapacitate their own movements. They collapsed in a tangle of unraveling weave, defeated by techniques they'd been taught to use but never trained to defend against.

The mask came away to reveal a face that belonged on someone no older than Amara—a young woman whose eyes held the hollow look of someone who'd been stripped of everything. She hadn't just been trained to kill; she'd been hollowed out and remade into a weapon wearing a human face.

Mute, Caedric observed, noting the surgical scars that marked where her tongue had been removed to prevent the possibility of confession under interrogation. Additional marks showed where the Hemlock sigil had been burned directly into her flesh, while an oath-brand sealed her forehead with symbols that bound her to Guild service.

They didn't just recruit her, he understood with growing horror. *They created her. Turned a person into an instrument.*

"Can you read what's been stitched into her clothing?" he asked Amara, studying the assassin's garments for hidden messages that might reveal intelligence about their deployment or objectives.

Amara approached with obvious reluctance, her hands trembling as she prepared to use techniques that might trigger responses from the tether that bound her to the Weaver. But necessity overcame fear—they needed information that only her gift could provide, regardless of what prices its use might demand.

A cloth materialized beneath her fingers, woven from threads that could make possibility manifest. Not normal fabric, but something that could translate magical resonances into patterns that normal senses could interpret.

"The Threadmarked must not reach the Looming Gate," she read, tracing symbols that had been stitched into the assassin's inner cloak lining with thread that glowed faintly in response to her touch.

The Looming Gate. The name suggested a location of significance. Not just another city marked on prophecy maps, but a destination that represented something crucial to the larger conflict.

"They fear what I might become," Amara said.

The observation was accurate, but it missed the larger picture that Caedric's training had taught him to recognize. Fear motivated the Guild's escalation, but it was a specific fear—not of what she was, but of what she might accomplish if allowed to reach what awaited at the destination that gave the Looming Gate its importance.

"They fear what you already are," he said, meeting her eyes. "This Looming Gate. Do you know what it is?"

"No."

"If the Guild believes it's worth deploying their most valuable assets to protect... that means it's exactly where we need to go."

CHAPTER 11
Amara

Myralis rose from the mountainside like something carved by patient hands over countless generations—not built so much as coaxed from the stone, its terraced levels ascending toward peaks that caught morning light and held it like precious thread. Ancient weaving runes marked the massive gates that controlled access to each district, their surfaces worn smooth by centuries of touch from travelers seeking the blessing of safe passage.

This is what we're fighting to preserve, Amara thought. *Places where people built according to a greater vision.*

The guards who controlled the lower gate studied them with suspicion that had been honed by recent events—not the casual wariness that came from routine duties, but the sharp attention of people who'd learned that strangers might carry dangers less visible than conventional weapons.

"State your business," commanded the senior guard, her hand resting on a sword hilt while her eyes tracked every movement Caedric made. "Myralis doesn't welcome refugees from Guild conflicts."

We're not refugees, Amara wanted to say. *We're messengers carrying a warning.* But the words felt hollow even before she could speak them. What were they if not people fleeing from forces too vast to face on their own?

She pushed back the hood of her traveling cloak. The silver scars along her arms caught the sunlight and threw it back in patterns that shifted with each angle of observation. The guard's expression transformed from suspicion to recognition.

"The Threadmarked," she breathed. The title made Amara's stomach clench with familiar discomfort. "We'd heard rumors, but..."

"I need to speak with your leaders," Amara said, keeping her voice steady despite the urge to deny the title that had been thrust upon her. "Danger is coming."

The guard's hand fell away from her sword. "I'll send word to the Council. They'll want to see you immediately."

The Council of Looms met in a chamber carved from the mountain's heart, its walls lined with tapestries that depicted the city's history. Twelve figures sat in a semicircle around a central loom that served as both a symbol and a practical workspace. They weren't rulers in the traditional sense, but representatives of craft guilds and civic organizations that had learned to govern through consensus rather than imposed authority.

Amara spread the prophecy tapestry fragment on the council table, its torn edges and bloodstains speaking of a journey that had tested more than physical endurance. The gold-threaded runes that marked cities deemed significant still pulsed with their own inner light, including the symbol that represented Myralis itself.

"Wraithstitchers are coming," she said, her voice carrying across the chamber despite its vast dimensions. "The Guild follows them, though not to stop their corruption but to claim the territories they leave broken. You've been marked by powers that care nothing for your independence or your survival."

Silence greeted her warning, but it wasn't the comfortable quiet of people considering new information. It was the tense hush that preceded rejection.

"Fables," declared a councilor whose robes bore the marks of merchant guild authority. "Stories told to frighten children and justify Guild expansion. The Threadmarked is a myth, not prophecy made flesh."

"I've seen the burned halls of Feymont," Amara replied, fighting to keep frustration from her voice. "Watched communities reduced to ash because they didn't believe the warnings. You can dismiss me as fable if you choose—but the Guild won't care what you believe when their purification units arrive."

"And how do we know," another councilor interjected, leaning forward with narrowed eyes, "that you're not simply a Guild agent sent to soften our defenses? Create panic, make us abandon the independence we've maintained for centuries?"

Caedric stepped forward. "I was a Guild enforcer for seven years. I know their tactics, their strategies, their methods of control." His voice was calm and measured. "What's coming for you isn't a political maneuver. It's annihilation wearing the mask of purification."

"A traitor's word," the merchant councilor spat. "Why should we trust—"

"Enough."

The single word cut through the rising argument like a blade through silk. An elderly councilor near the chamber's far end stirred, her blind eyes turning toward Amara with the unsettling accuracy of someone who'd learned long ago how to navigate the world without relying on sight. Deep scars marked her cheeks in patterns that spoke of ritual purposes, and her robes bore symbols that predated the Guild.

"There is an old tale," she said, her voice carrying clearly despite her age. "Passed down through oral tradition because it was too dangerous to preserve in thread or text.

The Threadmarked—a weaver born in flame, destined to either unbind or bind the world forever." She paused, and Amara felt the weight of those sightless eyes upon her. "We thought it a myth. A cautionary story about the dangers of unchecked power. Now I fear it might be a memory—knowledge of what came before, preserved through generations as a warning about what might come again."

The chamber fell silent. Even the skeptical merchant councilor had gone still, his earlier certainty wavering in the face of the elder's words.

"You've seen the marks on her arms," the old woman continued. "They aren't decorations. They're the physical manifestation of power that exists outside the Guild's carefully constructed hierarchy."

She turned her face toward the other councilors. "We can debate whether she is truly the figure from prophecy. But we cannot debate whether the threat she warns of is real. I have lived long enough to know the difference between political maneuvering and genuine apocalypse. This is the latter."

A younger councilor, wearing the insignia of the stonemasons' guild, spoke up. "Even if we believe the warning—and I'm not saying I do—what would you have us do? Myralis has stood independent for three hundred years precisely because we don't involve ourselves in conflicts between the Guild and its enemies."

"Your independence," Amara said quietly, "is about to become irrelevant. The Wraithstitchers don't negotiate. The Guild doesn't accept neutrality. When they come—if they aren't headed here now—you'll have to choose. The only question is whether you prepare now or wait until your choice is made in blood."

━━━◆━━━

The Loom Vault lay deeper in the mountain than seemed structurally possible, reached through passages that wound between natural caverns and ones carved by hands that had understood stone's essential nature. Its entrance was protected by wards that responded to the touch of blood mixed with thread—not preventing access, but ensuring that those who entered understood the sacred nature of what lay within.

The chamber itself was vast beyond the mountain's visible dimensions, filled with looms of every size and configuration. Some held half-completed works that waited for weavers who would never return to finish their designs, while others displayed tapestries so ancient that their threads had begun to dissolve back into the raw potential from which they'd been woven.

Ancestral memory, Amara understood, feeling a presence that had nothing to do with living consciousness. Echoes of everyone who'd worked in this space over centuries of careful practice, their intentions and techniques preserved in the very atmosphere that surrounded the stored artifacts.

Among the collection, one piece called to her with a pull that felt like recognition rather than mere attraction. A half-completed cloak depicted a figure she knew despite having never seen the work before—herself, standing before gates that burned with fire that consumed nothing while illuminating everything.

Without conscious decision, she reached toward the fabric.

The moment her fingers made contact, the sigils beneath her skin erupted with bone-light. Power flooded through pathways she'd never learned to navigate, completing the cloak's design with additions that spoke of futures she'd never contemplated before. The gates opened in the completed image, revealing transformation rather than destruction.

This is what you could accomplish, the tether whispered through her consciousness. *Not just warning people about dangers, but eliminating the possibility of danger through complete control over the threads that bind reality itself.*

The vision faded as quickly as it had appeared, leaving the cloak half-completed once more. But the memory remained, proof that her power was growing beyond boundaries she understood.

"Amara?" Caedric's voice cut through the lingering disorientation, concern sharp in his tone. "What just happened?"

She turned to find him studying her with an expression that mixed worry and something approaching fear—not of her, but *for* her, as he realized how difficult it was becoming to tell where she ended and the voices in her blood began.

"I don't know," she admitted, looking down at her hands that still tingled with residual power. "The vault's magic responded to something in me. Showed me possibilities I never wanted to see."

That night, unable to sleep despite the exhaustion that had settled into her bones, Amara found herself on one of Myralis's observation terraces. The city spread below in layers of light and shadow, beautiful in ways that made her chest ache with the weight of responsibility for its preservation.

Caedric joined her without announcement, his presence offering the kind of comfort that didn't require words or explanations. They stood together in silence, staring at the constellations overhead.

"Each city makes me feel more distant from myself," she said finally, giving voice to the fears that had been building since

Feymont. "Like I'm becoming the symbol they need rather than the person I actually am. What if the prophecy isn't leading me to freedom? What if it's just guiding me toward becoming exactly what the bone mirror showed?"

The question hung between them, sharp with implications. Every community that looked to her for salvation, every individual who pinned their hopes on her abilities—all of it pushed her toward accepting power that promised transcendence through corruption.

"They keep calling me a savior," she continued, her voice barely above a whisper. "What if I'm just the spark that burns it all down?"

Caedric was quiet for a long moment, his silence feeling deliberate rather than the absence of a response.

"You still choose what kind of thread you weave," he finally said. "The prophecy might show destinations, but the path between here and there belongs to you. Every decision is yours, not predetermined by forces that claim to know your purpose better than you do."

The reminder felt like an anchor against the currents that sought to pull her toward oblivion. Not because it solved the deeper clash between her will and the forces no one could truly control, but because it affirmed that some choices were still hers—no matter what powers tried to lay claim to her.

◆

Dawn brought news. A scout arrived at the council chamber with information that drained color from the faces that had been arguing about theoretical threats the day before.

"Guild warships," he reported, his voice tight with barely controlled panic. "Three full companies, moving upriver toward Myralis. They'll reach the lower terraces within two days."

The council erupted into chaos—some demanding immediate surrender to avoid the fate that had befallen Feymont, others calling for evacuation of the city's most vulnerable, still others insisting that fortifications could hold against any force the Guild might deploy.

Through the tumult, Amara felt eyes turning toward her. Not seeking her opinion as one voice among many, but looking for guidance from someone they'd already decided represented their best hope for survival.

This is the moment, she understood with crystalline clarity. *Where I either accept the role that's been thrust upon me, or watch another community burn because I was too afraid of what leadership might cost.*

The blind councilor's voice cut through the debate with authority. "If we stand with you, Threadmarked, will you stand with us?"

The question wasn't just an inquiry about military support. It was asking whether she'd accept responsibility for their fates, whether she'd become the symbol they needed even knowing what that transformation might cost.

Amara rose, feeling the weight of countless eyes tracking her movement. Not just the council, but the broader awareness that came from knowing entire communities were watching to see what choices she would make.

"I won't run," she said, her voice carrying across the chamber. "Not from the Guild, not from fate, not from whatever the prophecy claims I'm meant to become. I'll stand, and if I fall, let it be on my own terms, protecting people who deserve the chance to choose their own paths rather than accepting what others decide is best for them."

The vow felt like stepping off a cliff into darkness, trusting that purpose would provide the strength necessary to survive the impact that awaited at the bottom. But it was hers to make, her commitment to a cause that mattered more than individual survival.

Around the council chamber, she watched faces shift from uncertainty toward something approaching hope—not the naive optimism that believed her presence guaranteed victory, but the harder recognition that some battles were worth fighting regardless of their ultimate outcome.

The Threadmarked, she thought, accepting the title with all its implications and responsibilities. *Not because I wanted to become a symbol, but because people need symbols when reality offers only choices between bad options and worse ones.*

The Guild was coming, bringing forces designed to eliminate resistance. But Myralis wouldn't face them alone, and perhaps that would make the difference between survival and the kind of destruction that eliminated communities from history itself.

The Guild would bring siege and suffering that would test everyone who'd chosen to stand rather than flee. But right now, protected by stone walls and ancient wards and the fragile hope that unity might prove stronger than fear, they could prepare for battles that would determine whether independence remained possible in a world that seemed determined to eliminate everything beautiful or free.

Amara had made her choice. Now the Guild would have to face the consequences of pushing her too far.

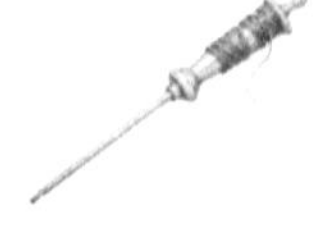

CHAPTER 12
Caedric

From the rooftop where he'd positioned himself to observe approach routes the Guild forces might use, Caedric watched Myralis transform itself into something between a fortress and a sanctuary. Families carried supplies into cellars that had been carved deep enough to withstand siege bombardment, while weavers moved through the streets reinforcing walls and buildings with protection sigils that glowed faintly in the twilight.

The city's transformation had begun the moment Amara made her vow to stand with them—not a gradual shift, but immediate mobilization as if her acceptance of leadership had released energy that had been waiting for direction. People who'd been paralyzed by uncertainty found purpose in preparation, communities that had been divided by disagreement discovered unity in their shared commitment to survival.

She threads the hope of others into herself, he realized, watching distant figures move through streets that would soon become battlegrounds. *But who unknots her when the weight becomes too heavy to bear alone?*

The question felt increasingly urgent as he considered how much she'd been carrying since Feymont—the burden of becoming a symbol rather than an individual, the weight of expectations from people who looked to her for solutions, the growing influence of forces that sought to claim her for their own purposes.

She's close to breaking, he understood with the clarity that came from having watched her struggle through weeks of mounting pressure. *And I don't know how to help her except by standing close enough to catch her if she falls.*

He found her in the Loom Vault, sitting cross-legged before the half-completed cloak. Her hands trembled as they worked thread through fabric that seemed to resist her efforts, while tears tracked down her cheeks that she didn't bother to wipe away. The scene struck him with such force that he paused, taking in her raw suffering.

"Amara?" He approached carefully, not wanting to startle her. "What are you trying to do?"

She looked up, her eyes red from exhaustion that had accumulated over weeks of insufficient rest. "Adding a thread of peace to the pattern. Something that might counterbalance the prophecy claims I'm meant to become. But it keeps fraying, like the design won't accept anything that contradicts its fundamental nature."

The explanation carried weight beyond its simple description—not just technical difficulty with threadwork, but that some patterns might be too deeply woven to alter through individual effort, no matter how skilled or determined.

He settled beside her on the vault's stone floor, close enough that their shoulders nearly touched. "You don't have to carry all of this alone. The leadership, the hope, the fear of becoming what the bone mirror showed you—

these burdens weren't meant for single people to bear."

"But I'm the Threadmarked," she said, her voice carrying the bitter recognition of the title that had been thrust upon her. "The one the prophecy marked for whatever role it's decided I should play. If I break under the weight, what happens to everyone who's counting on me to remain strong enough to guide them?"

The question revealed fears that went deeper than concerns about her immediate survival. It exposed anxieties about fundamental identity, about the distinction between becoming what circumstances required and losing everything that made individual existence meaningful.

"I don't know how to be myself anymore," she admitted, her hands falling still against the uncooperative fabric. "Every choice I make gets interpreted through the lens of what the Threadmarked should do rather than what I want. It's like I'm disappearing into the symbol, and soon there won't be anything left of the person I was before this all started."

Caedric felt something crack inside his chest. Not pain exactly, but the kind of breaking that preceded change into something stronger. He'd been carrying his own fears for weeks, his own concerns about what her growing power might cost, his own desperate hope that somehow they'd find ways to preserve what mattered most despite those bent on destruction.

"I'm terrified," he said, giving voice to truths he'd been holding close since the bone mirror vision had shown him how easily she might be lost to corruption. "Not of the Guild, though they're dangerous enough. Nor of the siege that's coming, though survival is far from certain. But of losing you—not to death, which would grieve me deeply, but to the transformation into something that wears your face while serving purposes you'd never choose."

Their eyes met across the small space between them, and for a moment all the careful professional distance they'd maintained dissolved into recognition of truths that had been growing clearer despite every effort to ignore them.

"If I unspool," she asked, her voice barely above a whisper, "who catches the thread?"

"I will," he replied without hesitation, the promise feeling like the most important vow he'd ever made. "Whatever happens, whatever you become, I'll be there to remind you of who you were before forces beyond your control decided what you should be."

They moved to the city walls as evening deepened into night. On the horizon, Guild banners rose like storm clouds gathering before the deluge, their organized arrangement speaking of military precision that would test Myralis's defenses beyond anything the city had been designed to withstand.

The tension in Caedric felt like physical pressure, building toward an expression that could no longer be contained. He'd been carrying the words for days—weeks, if he was honest about when his feelings had shifted from professional protection into something else.

Tell her, instinct demanded. *Before the siege, before circumstances make confession impossible, before you lose the chance to let her know what she means to you.*

He moved closer, their shoulders touching through layers of travel-worn fabric. His hand brushed hers where it rested on the stone parapet, the contact sending electricity through pathways that had nothing to do with thread-magic or supernatural influence.

She turned to face him, her expression vulnerable in ways she rarely allowed, eyes searching his face for meanings that words hadn't yet made explicit.

"There's something I need to say—" he began, the confession finally rising past the barriers that had kept it contained through weeks of mounting pressure.

She collapsed before Caedric could finish his sentence, gasping as something else seized control of her awareness. Her eyes glazed over with the familiar pale light that signaled the Weaver's intrusion, while threads from her traveling pack began to unravel and weave patterns that had nothing to do with her conscious will.

"Amara!" Caedric caught her as she fell, cradling her against his chest while calling her name with desperation.

When she spoke again, her voice carried layers that belonged to someone else entirely—the Weaver of Bone, speaking through the tether with coherence that suggested growing control over the connection that bound him to her.

"She is mine," the words emerged from her throat with harmonics that made Caedric's skin crawl. *"She opens every time she weaves, creates pathways I can follow back to her consciousness. You hold her hand, but I hold her soul."*

The taunting carried the truth that Caedric had been trying not to acknowledge— every time Amara used her gift beyond basic techniques, every moment she pushed her power to accomplish what normal threadwork couldn't achieve, she created connections that strengthened rather than weakened the tether's influence.

"Let her fall, Unraveler," the Weaver continued, his satisfaction evident even through the distortion of speaking through

another's voice. *"Or fall with her. Either way, she becomes what I've shaped her to be."*

No, Caedric thought with clarity that cut through his panic. *I won't let you have her. I won't let her become what you've decided she should be.*

Without conscious decision, his hands moved to the half-completed cloak that still lay beside them, his fingers finding the thread and needle. He'd never learned threadwork formally—his Guild training had focused on identifying and eliminating corruption rather than creating anything new.

But memory served purposes beyond mere recollection. And in this moment, he needed to create rather than destroy. The pattern he wove was simple, lacking the technical sophistication that years of practice would have provided. Just images that captured their first meeting.

Not perfect threadwork, he acknowledged, watching the crude stitches take shape beneath his fingers. *But honest. Real. Mine rather than something imposed by prophecy or corruption.*

As he worked, he spoke—not to the Weaver whose influence had displaced her consciousness, but to the part of Amara still existed beneath the possession that sought to claim her entirely.

"Remember who you were," he said, his voice steady despite hands that trembled with effort. "Before prophecy, before the tether, before you became the symbol others needed. Remember the woman who cut her own palm just to feel pain she could choose, who stood with communities despite knowing it might cost her everything."

The threadwork pattern grew beneath his fingers, images capturing not just their meeting but the choices she'd made since— every moment she'd chosen preservation over power, every decision to warn rather than command, every acceptance of limitation rather than transcendence through corruption.

This is who you are, the pattern declared. *Not what prophecy claims, not what power offers, but the person who chooses her own path despite every force that seeks to impose different destinations.*

Amara gasped, consciousness returning with a sudden violence that left her shaking in his arms. The pale light faded from her eyes, replaced by her natural color—still marked by exhaustion and fear, but recognizably her own rather than a mask worn by something else.

"Caedric?" Her voice was weak but present. "What... what happened?"

"The Weaver tried to claim you again," he said, holding her close while relief washed over him in waves that left him trembling almost as badly as she was. "But you came back. You're stronger than whatever he's trying to make you become."

But even as he spoke the words, he watched her expression shift from relief to something approaching despair. Not because she'd been possessed—that had happened before—but because she understood what the intrusion meant for their immediate future.

"Every time I stitch, I feel him," she said, tears streaming down her face. "I don't want to become him. I don't want to lose myself."

The confession carried not just fear of possession, but the recognition that her growing power came with prices that might prove too high to pay. *She's breaking,* Caedric understood, watching someone who'd been carrying impossible burdens finally reach the limits of what any individual could sustain. *And I don't know how to fix this except by sharing the weight in whatever ways she'll allow.*

"Then let me carry part of the thread," he said, the words emerging with conviction that surprised him. "We'll bind your path together. Not because I can prevent the corruption, but because some weights were never meant to be borne alone."

It wasn't a solution. The tether would still grow stronger, the corruption would still demand its price. But some struggles couldn't be faced alone, and perhaps that was enough—two people choosing to stand together against forces neither could defeat on their own.

He didn't kiss her. The moment felt too raw, too vulnerable, too weighted with implications about the future that might never arrive. But the intimacy of their shared breaking, of promises made in full knowledge of what they might ultimately cost, created a bond that went beyond simple romance.

Whatever comes next, Caedric thought, holding her while she grieved, *we face it together. Love doesn't guarantee victory, but it's worth fighting for regardless of whether we survive the battle.*

Tomorrow would bring siege and suffering, choices that would test everyone who'd decided to stand rather than flee. But tonight, protected by stone walls and fragile hope, they could rest.

Amara wept in his arms while Guild forces gathered on the horizon, preparing to eliminate all resistance. But she didn't weep alone.

CHAPTER 13
Amara

Dawn broke over Myralis like a wound opening in the sky—red light spilling across terraced stone as Guild forces descended from the surrounding hills. Hundreds strong, their ranks moved in disciplined formations while siege engines rolled into position.

From the command center carved into the mountain's heart, Amara watched the deployment through observation ports that offered strategic vantage without exposure to enemy fire. She wasn't hiding from the conflict but positioning herself where she could serve beyond combat.

This is what it means to be the Threadmarked, she thought, studying enemy positions with attention she'd never learned but somehow possessed. *Not just fighting, but giving others the framework to fight effectively.*

Caedric stood across the chamber, dividing his attention between the eastern approaches he'd been assigned to defend and her position near the council table. His expression carried concern.

"The eastern gate is their obvious target," he said, tracing approach routes on the map spread before them. "I'll position our strongest defenders there, but we need to assume they'll test every weakness simultaneously."

Around them, the Council of Looms fractured along fault lines that had been forming since her arrival. Half the councilors wanted to surrender, their voices sharp with fear that had overcome the principles that had once guided their governance. The others stood with her.

"We can't win against these numbers," declared the merchant councilor who'd called her a fable. "Surrender now, negotiate terms that might preserve some measure of autonomy—"

"They don't negotiate," Amara cut him off. "They eliminate. Feymont tried to surrender and was burned anyway. The Guild isn't here to accept our submission. They're here to erase any proof that resistance was ever possible."

The truth of her words hung in the air. This wasn't about winning in conventional military terms—the Guild's forces were too numerous, too well-equipped, too committed to destruction for simple victory to be achievable.

But there were other forms of success.

"We fight," she said, meeting the eyes of each councilor in turn. "Not to win outright, but to show people across the region that resistance *is* possible. To prove that the Guild's authority can be challenged. I refuse to accept that survival requires the surrender of everything that makes life meaningful."

"They want fear," she continued, feeling conviction rise past her doubts and anxieties that had been accumulating since Feymont. "Let's give them fire instead."

———◆———

The master weavers of Myralis gathered in the Loom Vault, their skilled hands ready to serve. They weren't creating art for its own sake, but channeling generations of accumulated knowledge into practical enchantments that might tip the balance between survival and destruction.

Amara worked beside them, her gift amplifying their techniques. The first banner warded against fire, its patterns creating barriers that would deflect alchemic flames before they could ignite the city's wooden structures. Another muffled sound, allowing troop movements to remain hidden from enemy observation.

For a young scout who volunteered to slip behind enemy lines and gather intelligence about Guild deployment patterns, she personally wove a cloak of shadowthread—fabric that absorbed light rather than reflecting it, making the wearer difficult to track even under direct observation.

As her hands moved through the familiar rhythms of creation, she felt the Weaver's whisper attempting to assert itself. Thread began to transform beneath her fingers, cotton shifting toward bone-white filaments. The sensation was subtle at first, easy to dismiss as exhaustion or stress, but she recognized it for what it was—the tether attempting to guide her.

No, she thought with crystalline clarity, burning away the transformed thread through an act of will. The bone-thread dissolved back into normal fiber, eliminated by sheer determination.

I need my own pattern, she realized, watching the other weavers work according to techniques that had been passed down through generations. *Something that belongs entirely to me rather than being inherited from Guild doctrine or the Weaver's vision.*

Without conscious decision, she began to chant—not words exactly, but sounds that carried meaning older than language. It was a threadsong that emerged from someplace deep within her consciousness.

The other weavers paused in their work, drawn by harmonics that seemed to resonate with the vault's ancestral memory. It wasn't a command for their attention, but an invitation to participate in creation.

This is mine, the song declared with each syllable.

The threadsong was still echoing in her bones when the first explosion shook the vault's foundations. Dust cascaded from ancient stone as the master weavers exchanged worried glances. A runner burst through the doorway, breathless and wide-eyed.

"The outer gate! It's beginning to fail!"

Amara's hands stilled over the half-finished banner in her lap. Around her, the other weavers looked to her with expressions that mingled hope and fear, waiting for direction. She set aside her work and rose, her legs protesting after hours spent kneeling at the loom.

"Continue the enchantments," she told the master weavers. "Every banner, every ward—it all matters. I need to see what we're facing."

The climb to the central tower seemed longer than it should have, each stone step carrying her higher above the city. Through narrow windows, she caught glimpses of the battle below. Defenders scrambling, barriers crumbling, the inexorable advance of Guild forces.

The outer gate began to splinter under sustained bombardment from the Guild's siege engines, its ancient wood proving insufficient against their weapons. Through the observation ports, Amara watched defenders scramble to reinforce barriers that were failing faster than they could be repaired.

Time to become what they need me to be, she thought. The gathered defenders looked up as she emerged onto the tower's observation platform, their faces showing exhaustion mixed with desperate hope that her appearance might herald some turning point in battle that had been slowly grinding toward an inevitable conclusion. She was in the open, which made her vulnerable to enemy fire, but visibility was the point. Leadership required being seen.

What do I say to people who are dying for choices I made? she wondered, studying faces that belonged to individuals with their own stories, their own reasons for standing when flight would have been safer. *How do I justify asking them to continue fighting when I can't promise victory?*

But honesty had always served her better than false comfort.

"We are not born for chains," she began, her voice carrying across the plaza. "Every thread they tried to cut, we knotted back together. Every community they attempted to silence, we gave voice through our defiance."

Below her, she watched the defenders— bloodied, exhausted, afraid, but still standing—begin to straighten as her words stirred their courage.

"They fear us," she continued, feeling truth settle around her shoulders like a mantle. "Not because we're stronger or more numerous, but because we know how to mend what they've spent generations trying to break. Because we remember that communities existed before Guild authority, and we refuse to accept that their vision of order is the only possibility."

The speech wasn't rehearsed or carefully calculated. It was a raw expression of everything she'd been learning. She raised the banner she'd been weaving, a standard that bore the flame-and-loom sigil that had become associated with her name, worked in threads that gleamed with more than reflected light. Not Guild heraldry or ancient symbols borrowed from traditions she didn't fully understand, but something that belonged to this moment, this choice, this refusal to accept what others said was inevitable.

"Let this thread run red or golden," she declared, planting the standard where it would be visible to defenders and enemies alike. "But let it run free!"

The Guild launched its full assault. Ballista bolts targeted structural weaknesses, alchemic fire sought to ignite anything flammable, and waves of arrows darkened the air, falling in relentless volleys meant to eliminate defenders before ground forces moved forward.

The eastern gate shattered completely, and Guild soldiers poured through the breach. *We can't hold,* Amara realized, watching defensive lines begin to collapse under pressure. *Not through conventional means, not against these numbers and their weapons.*

But even as the thought formed, she saw movement at the breach—Caedric emerging from the smoke and chaos with a small group of fighters whose uniforms bore Guild insignia despite their presence on Myralis's side of the conflict.

Defectors, she understood with growing amazement. *Weavers who saw the banner and chose to abandon the forces they'd been serving. They must have seen it and remembered why they learned threadwork in the first place.*

The defecting weavers moved through Myralis's defensive positions with knowledge of Guild tactics that made them invaluable for countering strategies they'd been trained to employ. Not enough to guarantee victory, but sufficient to transform inevitable defeat into something approaching a stalemate.

One final push, Amara thought, feeling exhaustion that had accumulated over hours of sustained magical effort. *One more weaving to give us the chance we need.*

The bridge that connected the market district to the main plaza had been battered by Guild bombardment, preventing reinforcements from reaching positions where they were desperately needed. Normal repair would take hours they didn't have, require resources that weren't available in the midst of active combat.

But she'd stopped limiting herself to normal techniques weeks ago.

Drawing on reserves from where she hadn't thought to look, Amara reached for the bridge with senses that existed beyond normal perception. Not seeing the physical structure, but feeling the threads that had once bound stone to stone, understanding the pattern that had made the bridge functional before violence had torn it apart.

Mend, she commanded. *Remember what you were and become it again.*

Stone flowed like liquid thread, reforming according to designs that had been disrupted but not entirely destroyed. The bridge rebuilt itself in moments, its ancient strength restored. Reinforcements surged across the repaired structure, their arrival shifting the tactical balance from desperate defense to effective resistance.

The siege didn't end in total victory, though. The Guild forces were too numerous for complete defeat, and Myralis's defenders were too exhausted to pursue enemies that withdrew toward regrouping positions. But it ended in survival, which felt like triumph after hours of combat that had seemed destined to conclude with the city's systematic destruction.

Word spread through enchanted thread-carriers before the last enemy soldier had retreated beyond bowshot range: *Myralis held. The Threadmarked stands. The Guild can be resisted.*

As evening settled over the battered city, messages began arriving from communities that had been watching the outcome. They didn't just express solidarity but declared their own intentions to stand rather than surrender when Guild forces arrived to their gates.

The thread is spreading, Amara realized, watching responses accumulate faster than they could be properly catalogued. *Not just hope, but actual coordination between communities that had been isolated by fear.*

She walked through broken battlements as darkness claimed the day, studying damage that would take months to fully repair. Bodies lay where they'd fallen—both defenders and Guild soldiers, individuals whose stories had been reduced to casualties in a conflict.

Caedric joined her among the wounded. They were being tended by healers who worked with supplies stretched beyond normal limits. They stood together in silence. His hand found hers, their fingers intertwining with careful intimacy.

"You gave them more than a city," he said quietly. "You gave them a thread of hope. Proof that the Guild's authority can be challenged by the common folk."

They'd survived, but the Weaver was still watching, she knew, feeling the tether pulse with interest as it registered her use of power. *Every weaving pulls me closer to whatever he's decided I should become.*

But she'd also discovered something crucial during the battle—her own threadsong, a pattern that belonged entirely to her. It wasn't complete protection against corruption, but it was better than nothing.

The Guild would respond to this defeat with escalation, the Weaver would continue his patient corruption, and communities across the region would look to her for guidance she still wasn't certain she could provide.

But standing among the ruins of battle that had been survived rather than won, holding hands with someone who'd chosen to stand beside her despite every reason to walk away, she could briefly rest in the knowledge that some threads ran true regardless of what forces sought to tangle or cut them.

The banner she'd planted still flew above the central tower, its flame-and-loom sigil visible even in the darkness. Not just her standard, but a symbol for everyone. She had given them hope. Now she needed to learn how to weave that hope into something strong enough to survive what came next.

CHAPTER 14
Caedric

Caedric sat in what had been designated as the resistance command center, sorting through messages that ranged from formal pledges of support to simple repetitions of a single word: Threadmarked. Threadmarked. Threadmarked.

Harrowfen, a textile city known for producing the finest wool in the region, sent coded assurances that their looms stood ready to support whatever the resistance required. Vireth, a mountain settlement that had maintained independence through careful diplomacy, declared their willingness to provide sanctuary for refugees displaced by Guild retaliation.

But one scroll caught his attention with contents that made his stomach clench— bloodstained thread wrapped around words that spoke of actions already taken: *We burned the tapestries. What now?*

They're moving before we're ready to support them, he realized, studying messages that suggested spontaneous uprisings spreading faster than any coordinated effort could manage. *They're inspired by Myralis's survival but they're acting without the resources or strategic planning that made our defense successful.*

The rebel council that had formed in the days following the siege gathered around the table where he'd spread the most significant messages. They weren't formal leadership in the traditional sense, but representatives of groups that had learned to coordinate through necessity rather than imposed hierarchy—ex-weavers who'd defected from Guild service, hedge-stitchers whose informal practices had been targeted for elimination, farmers whose communities had been destroyed by purification campaigns, even a few sympathetic nobles whose estates had been seized when they'd refused to support Guild expansion.

"It's not just a fire now," observed Maela, the former stitch-librarian from Feymont who'd become one of the resistance's key coordinators. "It's a tapestry unraveling. Every thread we pull affects patterns we can't fully see."

She wasn't wrong, but her comparison overlooked details Caedric's Guild training had taught him to notice. Unraveling could transform or destroy. The difference often came down to whether anyone was prepared to guide the process toward a constructive outcome.

While Amara rested in chambers deep within the mountain—exhausted by magical exertion that had pushed her gift beyond sustainable limits—Caedric found himself stepping into roles he'd never expected to occupy. Not just military strategy, which aligned with his Guild training, but the broader organizational work that transformed scattered resistance into something approaching a coordinated movement.

He established messenger networks using conventional tradecraft with magical communication methods shared by the defecting weavers. It wasn't a centralized command structure that would create vulnerable points of failure, but a distribution systems where each node could operate independently while contributing to a larger coordination.

Sympathetic weavers who'd joined the resistance after witnessing Myralis's stand worked under his direction to produce specialized equipment—cloaks threaded with anti-scrying enchantments that made wearers difficult to track through Guild truth-reading, armor that bore resistance sigils capable of deflecting magical attacks, banners that could serve as rallying points while broadcasting coded messages to those who knew how to read them.

And in sessions that would have been considered treasonous during his Guild service, he shared his knowledge with others, including basic unraveling methods, how to sever surveillance wards without triggering alarms that would alert Guild monitors, ways to detect false threads that had been woven to mislead resistance efforts, and to identify

Guild agents who'd been placed within communities to report on seditious activities.

I hunted weavers like these, he thought, watching students practice the techniques he'd once employed to eliminate them. *Now I'm teaching them.*

The change should have troubled him. It was evidence of how completely he'd abandoned principles that had once defined his understanding of duty and honor. Instead, it felt like the truth finally acknowledged, like stepping out of shadows into light that revealed what had always existed beneath carefully maintained facades.

This is what I was meant to do, he realized. *Not enforcing compliance, but helping people develop the skills necessary to make their lives meaningful.*

The news from Faldris arrived during an afternoon coordination session, delivered by a rider whose horse had been pushed beyond its limits to bring information that couldn't wait for slower but safer communication methods.

Razed, the message declared with brutal simplicity. *New Wraithstitchers wearing bone-threaded cloaks. They used twisted spellweaving that turned defensive wards into traps. A child's cloak was used as an anchor point to spread fire through the entire settlement.*

Survivors spoke of horrors that made the Bone Cloister's practices seem restrained by comparison. Not just killing, but corruption that transformed their victims into components of larger magical workings. Buildings that burned with flames that fed on life itself rather than conventional fuel. Wards that had been designed to protect instead serving to trap families in structures that became their funeral pyres.

They declared loyalty for Amara, Caedric understood, reading between the sparse details to comprehend the picture. *And the Guild made them an example.*

Rage rose within him, pushing him into the territory where emotion threatened to override tactical consideration. These weren't abstract casualties or acceptable losses in larger conflicts—they were people who'd made choices inspired by watching Myralis stand, who'd trusted that the resistance would protect them from the retaliation they couldn't face alone.

And we failed them, the truth cut deeper than any blade. *Not through malice or incompetence, but through the inability to be everywhere at once, to protect everyone who needs protection.*

He was halfway to the stables before conscious thought caught up with his emotions. There was no plan beyond riding toward Faldris and making someone pay for what had been done to people whose only crime was believing in something other than the Guild.

"Caedric." Amara's voice stopped him. She was still pale from her exertion, still marked by exhaustion that went beyond physical fatigue, but present when he needed the kind of grounding that only she could provide.

"They burned children," he said, the words emerging with grief that had been building since Feymont. "Used their clothing as magical anchors to spread fire through an entire settlement. And we're supposed to just accept that we can't retaliate?"

"We don't fight with fire," she replied. "We mend. We protect. We give people alternatives to accepting that cruelty is the only response to cruelty."

The distinction was important despite the rage that demanded satisfaction through violence. Fighting with fire meant becoming what they opposed and accepting that systematic destruction was appropriate when employed against enemies rather than allies. But mending required different methods, different understanding of what victory might actually mean.

She's right, he acknowledged, though the recognition did nothing to diminish the anger that sought outlet through action. *Retaliation would feel satisfying, but it would accomplish nothing except proving that we're no different from those we're fighting.*

———◆———

The scroll from Veradan arrived unsealed—not because security had been compromised, but because its contents were meant to be shared widely rather than restricted to resistance leadership. A major city, and former Guild stronghold where authority had seemed unshakeable, declaring that its people had overthrown the local Guild Hall and were holding public ceremonies to burn the tapestries that had symbolized Guild dominance.

We await the Threadwrought Queen, the message concluded in thread that had been dyed red.

"They see you as a queen now?" Caedric asked, watching Amara study the scroll with an expression of disbelief that bordered on horror.

She was quiet for a long moment, her fingers tracing the red thread that carried implications about how common people were interpreting her role in conflicts that had grown far beyond anything either of them had intended when their flight began.

"No," she said finally. "They see me as their thread of hope. Let's not let it snap."

Perhaps they didn't see her as a queen in the traditional sense, but rather a symbol that connected disparate communities.

This is what revolution actually looks like, Caedric thought, studying the message that suggested the momentum was building toward something neither the Guild nor the resistance could fully control. *This isn't organized campaigns following clear strategies, but spontaneous coordination emerging from thousands of individuals choosing to stand rather than submit.*

The recognition brought both hope and fear in equal measure. Hope that change might actually be possible, and fear that the unraveling tapestry might fall apart entirely.

That night, in the Loom Vault, Amara and Caedric shared the first quiet meal they'd managed since the siege. It wasn't a strategy session or tactical planning, just two people taking a brief respite from responsibilities that had grown beyond anything either could fully manage alone.

The food was simple. Bread and cheese salvaged from stores that had survived the battle and wine that tasted of distant vineyards where life continued normally. The companionship transformed the humble fare into something approaching luxury, presence mattering more than the provisions.

"Do you ever wonder what we'd be doing if none of this had happened?" Amara asked, the weariness evident in her voice. "If the Guild hadn't come for me, if you hadn't chosen to stand with me?"

The question invited speculation about alternate lives that might have been possible, futures that had been foreclosed when their paths intersected. But Caedric found he couldn't imagine those alternatives with any clarity. Not because his memory failed, but because the person he'd been before meeting her felt increasingly distant, like someone he'd known in passing rather than someone he'd actually been.

"I'd probably still be hunting people like you," he admitted. "Following orders, eliminating threats to authority, telling myself that individual suffering was acceptable when it served the larger good."

"And now?"

"Now I know that was a lie we told ourselves to avoid confronting what we were actually doing." He reached toward her cheek without conscious decision, drawn by the need to offer physical comfort that words couldn't adequately express.

She pulled away—not sharply, not with rejection, but a careful withdrawal that spoke of fears deeper than romantic involvement.

"If I let myself fall..." she began, the words trailing off.

"Then I fall with you," he replied. "Or catch you. Whichever proves necessary."

The moment lingered unresolved, charged with implications about futures that might never arrive and choices that couldn't yet be made. Not because they didn't understand what they felt for each other, but because circumstances demanded that some desires remain unacted upon until survival became something more than a daily struggle.

My loyalty isn't to the cause anymore, Caedric acknowledged. *It's to her. And whatever that means for the rebellion, whatever prices it demands from both of us, I'm committed to seeing this through to whatever end awaits.*

The spark had caught. Now they needed to learn how to guide the fire before the burning began.

CHAPTER 15
Amara

The forgotten Guild hall sat like a shadow in the mountainside, its entrance half-collapsed by centuries of neglect and deliberate obscuration. According to the message that had drawn them here, it predated the modern Guild by generations, built during the Weaver Wars when competing factions had fought for control over how magic would shape civilization.

A place where winners wrote history, Amara thought, studying stonework that bore marks of purposeful destruction. *Where one vision of order claimed supremacy by making all others impossible to practice.*

Their small group—herself, Caedric, Maela, and three rebels who'd defected from Guild service—descended through passages that wound between natural caverns and deliberately carved chambers. The air grew thick with dust and something else, a bitter scent that made Amara's throat tighten with recognition.

Burned thread, she identified, remembering the distinctive odor from purge sites she'd encountered. *This place witnessed violence.*

The Pattern Vault lay at the structure's deepest level, protected by wards that had degraded over centuries but still carried enough residual power to make Amara's scars pulse with warning. They didn't prevent entry, but instead announced that what lay within demanded respect from anyone who understood the fundamental nature of woven magic.

The chamber itself was vast beyond what the mountain's dimensions should have allowed, filled with scrolls that had begun to crumble into dust, tapestries whose threads had lost their color, tomes bound with materials that predated modern understanding. All of it dying slowly, knowledge being lost through simple neglect rather than active destruction.

But at the vault's center, preserved within a circle of standing stones, lay something that still hummed with active power.

The Prime Pattern was worked into animal hide that should have decayed centuries ago but remained supple as fresh leather, its surface marked with a circular glyph that seemed to shift and flow despite remaining fundamentally unchanged. It was a blueprint that defined how magic itself could be woven into lasting structures.

This is how they did it, Amara understood with growing horror, studying the patterns. *Not just creating spells or enchantments, but writing their authority into the fundamental fabric of how reality operates.*

"This... this is how they tethered us," she said, her voice barely above a whisper as recognition crystallized. "Not just with laws or military force, but with seams stitched into our very existence. Into clothing we wear, language we speak, even the memories we use to understand who we are."

Caedric moved around the Prime Pattern carefully, examining the details more thoroughly than Amara. Near the glyph's outer edge, worked in thread so fine it was nearly invisible, was a coded reference that made his expression darken.

"A subpattern," he said, tracing the symbols with a finger that didn't quite touch the hide's surface. "Embedded in every Guild apprentice's training cloak, creating a connection to the Prime Pattern that persists even after the physical garment is destroyed."

Sera, a teenage weaver who'd joined the resistance after watching her family's textile business be destroyed, approached the Prime Pattern.

"If you destroy it," she asked, voicing the question that had been building in Amara's own mind, "what happens to the magic we use? If everything is built on this foundation, does eliminating it mean we lose everything?"

I don't have an answer, Amara acknowledged silently, studying the Prime Pattern that hummed with power. *But I know it has to go. The foundation is too corrupt to build anything worthwhile upon, regardless of what gets lost in the demolition.*

They gathered materials from throughout the vault—oil that had been stored for preserving manuscripts, kindling from furniture that had survived centuries in the dry underground atmosphere, anything that might burn hot enough to destroy the hide that had been designed to resist normal damage.

As Amara laid her hands on the Prime Pattern to begin the work of severing its connections before the actual burning, the threads resisted her. They writhed beneath her touch like living things, while voices emerged from the glyph's depths—not just Guild doctrine, but something older and more familiar.

You cannot unmake legacy, the Weaver of Bone whispered through the pattern's resonance. *Power built over generations, authority woven into the fundamental nature of how communities organize themselves—these transcend individual will or choice.*

For a moment, she felt herself drawn toward the pattern's logic. Not because she wanted to preserve Guild authority, but because some part of her recognized truth in the Weaver's observation. Destruction was easier than creation, and what would replace the structure they were about to eliminate?

You're becoming what I want you to be, the voice continued. *Not a servant to existing powers, but an architect of alternatives that will require the same systematic control you claim to oppose.*

"No," she said aloud, the word carrying conviction that pushed past doubt and uncertainty. "I am not your vessel. I am the hand that severs."

She shouted her own name into the vault's darkness. Not Threadmarked or any other title that had been thrust upon her, but simply *Amara.* The sound echoed off the stones, weaving itself into the air with force.

The oil-soaked materials caught quickly once she applied flame, but the fire that consumed the Prime Pattern was unlike any normal combustion. The glyph screamed—not with sound exactly, but with vibrations. Tendrils of unraveling magic lashed out like threads being torn from a tapestry that someone was desperately trying to preserve, seeking purchase in anything that might anchor the pattern's continuation.

Caedric threw his cloak over her shoulders, shielding her from the magical backlash that would have burned anyone without protection. The gesture cost him—she saw the heat scorch his shoulder, but he held his position, a barrier between her and the fire.

Together they watched the Prime Pattern burn, its destruction releasing centuries of control back into raw potential. The screaming faded gradually, replaced by silence that felt simultaneously liberating and terrifying—absence of structure that had defined how magic operated for longer than anyone living could remember.

The aftershocks began within hours of their return to the camp outside Veradan. Weavers who'd been trained by the Guild reported strange sensations—some losing access to specific spell forms entirely, techniques they'd relied upon suddenly becoming impossible to execute. Others described feeling clearer, as if a fog that had been obscuring their perception had lifted without them realizing it had existed.

Amara felt both effects at once. Lighter, unburdened by connections she hadn't known were shaping her choices. But also hollow, as if something that had been part of her essential nature had been unknotted, leaving a space that needed to be filled.

Caedric found her at the camp's edge as evening settled over the mountain valleys, his shoulder bandaged where the magical backlash had burned through fabric and skin. He moved carefully, pain evident despite his attempts to project normal capability.

"While I hated the Guild," he said quietly, settling beside her, "some part of me still believed in structure, in the traditions that connected us to those who came before, even if those traditions had become corrupt."

"So did I," Amara replied. "But belief stitched into a cage isn't faith. It's a prison. And sometimes the only way to freedom requires burning everything down, even the parts that felt comfortable or familiar."

Rain began falling as full darkness claimed the day, its sound against burned silk creating rhythms that reminded Amara of her grandmother's weaving songs. Back in the tent they shared with other resistance leadership, she found herself tending to Caedric's wound with supplies salvaged from Guild stores they'd brought from Myralis.

The burn was serious but not life-threatening, blistered skin that would scar but heal with proper care. As she worked salve into the damaged tissue, she found herself acutely aware of their proximity—not just their physical closeness, but the emotional intimacy that had been building over the weeks they'd spent together.

His breathing changed as her fingers traced patterns around the wound's edges, not just treating the injury but acknowledging the sacrifice he'd made to shield her from the consequences of her choice.

Their eyes met, charged with the recognition of everything they'd been carefully not saying to each other. It wasn't because she didn't understand what she felt, but because circumstances had demanded those desires remain unacted upon.

He leaned forward, the movement slow enough that she could have pulled away if she'd wanted to. Instead, she reached out to touch his chest, not stopping his approach, but feeling the heartbeat beneath skin that bore scars from countless battles.

"Not yet," she said softly. "But soon."

The promise hung between them like thread waiting to be woven into patterns neither could fully envision. Not because she didn't want the connection that physical intimacy might create, but because some part of her recognized that crossing that threshold would change everything—transform their careful partnership into something that couldn't be undone if circumstances demanded different choices.

When this is over, she thought, studying his face in lamplight that painted features she'd grown to know better than her own. *When we've survived this war, when the immediate threats have been addressed, then we can explore what this might become.*

But the thought felt incomplete even as she formed it. Wars didn't end cleanly, revolutions didn't conclude with tidy resolutions, and the forces arrayed against them wouldn't simply accept defeat.

Reports arrived through the night. The Prime Pattern's destruction had sent ripples through the Guild and every community—communication spells faltering, coordination breaking down, some entire Guild facilities losing access to systems that had defined their operational capabilities.

But it had also awakened something else.

The Weaver of Bone, who'd been maintaining a relatively subtle influence through the tether that bound him to Amara's consciousness, suddenly surged with attention that felt like pressure building before a storm. He didn't speak words, but projected his satisfaction mixed with something approaching respect—recognition that she'd moved beyond being merely a defiant tool to become a genuine threat to everything his legacy represented.

You've chosen to burn rather than build upon what came before, the presence observed. *Now you must create alternatives from nothing but will and imagination. Let us see if you possess the strength that such creation demands.*

The challenge felt liberating. She'd eliminated the Guild's control mechanism, proven that their authority wasn't inevitable or unbreakable. But destruction was only the first step—now came the harder work of weaving new patterns that could serve human flourishing without recreating the very structures they'd fought to dismantle.

I'll invent something new, she promised herself, watching the rain fall. *Something that belongs to communities rather than institutions, that emerges from voluntary participation rather than imposed obligation.*

Whether that would prove possible, whether she possessed the knowledge and creativity necessary for such fundamental innovation, remained uncertain. But uncertainty felt preferable to the false confidence that came from building upon a corrupt foundation.

New challenges would arise as the Guild responded to losing their Prime Pattern, and the Weaver would continue his patient corruption, seeking to transform her into the architect of a new tyranny that might prove worse than what she'd destroyed.

But for now, she held onto the promise of "soon."

CHAPTER 16
Caedric

Night settled over the encampment with an uncomfortable weight. Caedric moved along the perimeter with vigilance, checking defensive positions that had been established after their return from the forgotten Guild hall.

Amara slept in the command tent, her body still recovering from the magical recoil that had followed the Prime Pattern's destruction. Exhaustion deeper than physical fatigue had claimed her within hours of their return, leaving her vulnerable and making Caedric's protective instincts sharpen into hyperawareness of every sound, every shadow, every detail that might herald approaching danger.

She burned the foundation of Guild authority, he reminded himself, studying the forest's edges where darkness gathered between the trees. *Of course they'll respond with everything they have.*

The silence struck him first. Not a peaceful quiet, but the eerie absence of sound. No wind rustled through leaves, no night birds called to each other, no small animals moved through the undergrowth. Just a stillness that felt imposed, as if something had silenced the forest.

One of the scouts emerged from the treeline at a run, her movements carrying panic that cut through the night's oppressive atmosphere. Thread bindings on their arms had been torn, leaving marks that spoke of a struggle and a narrow escape.

"They're coming," the scout gasped, breath ragged from exertion and fear. "The Guild. But not like before. Something's wrong with their soldiers—they move like puppets, like—"

Dark mist began creeping from the forest edge before her explanation could be completed, rolling across the ground with the deliberate purpose of something guided by conscious intent. It glowed faintly with patterns that resembled stitch-marks, and shapes began to materialize within its depths.

The Threadbound emerged like nightmares given form—human figures moving with the jerky precision of marionettes controlled by unseen hands, their mouths sewn shut with thread that gleamed like bone in the mist's unnatural illumination. Former weavers, rebels who'd been captured in previous engagements, even what appeared to be ex-Hemlock Circle members, all transformed into walking weapons.

They're being controlled, Caedric realized with horror. *Not just compelled or coerced, but literally puppeted through bone-thread runes etched directly into their skin.*

"To arms!" he shouted, his voice cutting through the shocked paralysis that had gripped the camp. "Defensive positions! Protect the command tent!"

The attack came with overwhelming numbers, the Threadbound moving as extensions of a single consciousness rather than independent fighters. They reached toward protective wards with hands that should have triggered defensive enchantments, but instead the magical barriers simply unraveled, their patterns coming apart at their touch.

Ensorcelled needles flew from their palms like thrown daggers, pinning garments—and the people wearing them—to the ground, trees, and tents with precision that spoke of inhuman aim. Where bone-thread touched, fire spells refused to ignite, defensive magic failed to activate, and the carefully prepared protections the camp had relied upon proved insufficient.

We can't fight them with normal weapons, Caedric understood, watching the defenders struggle. *We need to adapt, find their weaknesses rather than trying to overpower strengths we can't match.*

"Snag bombs!" he called to the rebels who'd been practicing with the improvised weapons they'd developed during training sessions. "Use the confusion devices. Don't try to kill them, just disrupt their coordination!"

The sacks of tangled thread enchanted to interfere with magical communication proved more effective than the protective wards.

When thrown into the clusters of Threadbound, they created zones of magical static that broke the precise coordination the puppeteers relied upon. They didn't destroy the enemies, but bought crucial seconds for the defenders to reposition and adapt to the assault.

Caedric moved through the chaos with his thread-cutter drawn, targeting the bone-thread runes that controlled the Threadbound rather than the victims themselves. Each severing released a puppet from external control, though the freedom often came with a fatal cost—bodies collapsing as the force had been animating them withdrew, leaving only the damaged remains of people who'd been transformed into weapons against their will.

I'm killing them to free them, the recognition cut deeper than any physical wound. *And there's no other option, no way to break the control without destroying what little remains of who they were.*

Sera's voice cut through the battle's din, young and defiant despite the terror that should have paralyzed someone with her limited combat experience. She'd joined the front line, wearing a cloak she'd stitched herself with hope-sigil threads.

"Get back!" Caedric shouted, watching her engage three Threadbound who'd broken through the defensive perimeter. "You're not trained for—"

But she was already moving, her cloak's enchantments deflecting ensorcelled needles while she wove counter-patterns that disrupted the bone-thread control enough to create openings for the other defenders. She didn't kill anyone, but held them at bay long enough for civilians to escape the collapsing defensive line.

She's buying time, he realized, recognizing her sacrifice even as he tried to push toward her position. *She knows she can't win, but she's creating the space others need to survive.*

The Wraithstitcher emerged from the mist with unhurried grace, his movements sending bone-thread lashing toward Sera, binding her arms before she could complete her defensive patterns.

Her scream was cut short as additional thread sewed itself through her lips. The Wraithstitcher dragged her backward into the fog, her eyes wide with terror. Caedric lunged forward, abandoning his position in a desperate attempt to reach her before she disappeared entirely. But hands grabbed his cloak, pulling him back with enough force to send him stumbling as bone-thread lashed through the space his body had occupied moments before.

"You can't save her," Amara's voice cut through his attempt to tear free and continue the pursuit. "Not without being taken yourself. And we need you here."

The words carried truth that logic recognized even as every instinct demanded he ignore it in favor of immediate rescue. But the fog was already dissipating, taking Sera and the Wraithstitcher with it, leaving only the chaos of ongoing battle.

Amara moved past him toward the fighting's center, her movements carrying exhaustion that should have prevented magical exertion but was being overridden by something darker than fury. She drew a bone needle from her pack, its surface yellowed with age. Caedric's Guild-trained instincts scream warnings.

No, he thought, recognizing the implement. *That's a blood-weaver's tool. She can't—*

But she was already working, her other hand drawing a small blade across her palm. Blood welled from the cut, and instead of falling to the ground, it rose into the air like thread being pulled from a spool.

She began to weave, and Caedric felt the earth itself respond. Not just the surface, but something deeper. She was pulling at the bones of the world that no Guild magic was supposed to touch.

A forbidden pattern, he realized with growing horror. *Who taught her this pattern?*

Bone-thread materialized, drawn from the memories embedded in the soil beneath their feet, centuries of death and decomposition transformed into material. She wove it together with her blood-thread, creating patterns that had been banned for good reason, techniques that operated on principles too dangerous for institutional oversight to permit.

"Amara, stop!" he called, but she was already too deep into the working to hear anything.

The bone needle flashed as she worked it through the earth itself, stitching patterns directly into the ground's substance. Each pass created visible seams in reality, lines where existence folded according to her intention rather than natural law.

She's treating the land like fabric, Caedric understood with awe that bordered on terror. *Weaving it as if it were cloth rather than stone and soil.*

The ground beneath the attacking Threadbound began to crack, fissures spreading with the deliberate precision of seams being opened by skilled hands. But instead of remaining open, the earth folded— closing on itself like a garment hem being finished, stone and soil flowing like liquid thread to trap the Threadbound within solid matter.

Dozens of them vanished as the ground swallowed them, their forms disappearing into the earth. No screams, no final cries— just silence as bodies were incorporated into substance that would hold them until erosion eventually returned their matter to the cycle that had produced it.

Some of the rebels screamed as they watched, horror overriding relief at the threat's elimination. This wasn't combat as they understood it, but something that resembled the Wraithstitchers' methods.

The magical aftershock hit like a physical blow, radiating from Amara with a force that sent Caedric stumbling despite his distance from the epicenter. She collapsed to her knees, her fingertips blackened by power that had burned through channels not meant to carry such intensity, while thread-patterns had seared themselves into her palms with permanent scarring that would mark her forever as someone who'd used techniques that should have remained forgotten.

The Guild forces withdrew as quickly as they'd arrived, melting back into the forest's darkness. But before the last enemy disappeared, Caedric saw them working on something—bone-thread being stitched into the bodies of the fallen.

When he reached the corpses after the retreat was complete, the words were clear despite being written in materials that made his stomach clench: *You burn patterns. We burn blood.*

———◆———

Dawn found the survivors moving among the wounded, struggling to reckon with losses that couldn't be measured by numbers alone. Bodies needed burial, injured required healing they might not survive, and the unknown fates of those like Sera were unlikely to be resolved in ways that offered comfort.

Caedric moved through the aftermath with the mechanical efficiency that came from having processed battlefield casualties too many times during his Guild service. Triage decisions about who could be saved and who was beyond help, practical considerations about resource allocation, tactical assessment of how the camp's defensive capabilities had been compromised.

But underneath the professional competence ran grief that had nothing to do with strategic calculation. Sera had been so young, so determined to prove herself useful despite lacking the combat training that might have saved her. And he'd failed to protect her, though not through incompetence or cowardice.

This is what leadership actually costs, he understood. *It's not just making hard decisions, but living with the consequences when those decisions reshape lives you never meant to harm.*

Amara found him among the wounded, her own exhaustion evident in her movements. She studied the message the Wraithstitchers had left, her expression shifting from horror to something approaching grim determination.

"They don't just want obedience anymore," she said, her tone flat. "They want annihilation. Complete elimination of everything."

Her observation was accurate. The Guild had decided that if they couldn't rule absolutely, they would ensure no one else could build anything worth ruling. *Total war,* Caedric recognized. *Not just a military conflict, but the kind of struggle where only complete victory or absolute defeat remains possible.*

The realization should have been paralyzing, but instead it felt like clarification. No more half-measures, no more hoping that limited resistance might achieve acceptable compromises. The Guild had made their choice—now the resistance needed to respond with equal commitment.

"We need to stop pretending restraint will save us," Amara continued, speaking to the gathered survivors. "The Guild must fall. Not reformed, not regulated, but eradicated completely."

The declaration felt like a line was being crossed, but this was a revolution rather than a reformation.

As the camp began the slow work of recovery and rebuilding, Caedric found himself sitting beside Amara on a ridge that overlooked the valley where the sun was beginning to paint the landscape in shades of gold and amber. Smoke still rose from burned sections of their defensive perimeter, while the wounded's cries provided counterpoint to the morning birds that had returned now that the unnatural silence had lifted.

She leaned against him without speaking, her head finding his shoulder. They weren't leaders right now planning their next moves, but simply two people who'd survived another night when survival had seemed unlikely.

This is what we're fighting for, he thought, feeling her warmth against his side. *Not abstract principles or political theories, but the simple ability to exist as ourselves rather than as instruments serving the Guild.*

The night siege had tested them in ways that went beyond simple combat, forcing them to realize what war actually demanded from those willing to fight. They'd survived, though survival had come at costs that would echo through what remained of their lives.

And perhaps that was enough. Not victory in conventional terms, but proof that resistance remained possible even when enemies deployed their most horrifying weapons, that communities could endure despite systematic attempts at elimination.

The threads Amara had woven in the ground still shimmered faintly, protecting the survivors who were beginning to emerge from hiding. It wasn't Guild magic, but something new—something born from loss, strengthened through shared determination, offering protection that emerged from human connection.

She's not just destroying what came before, Caedric understood. *She's creating alternatives, weaving something that might survive long enough to transform how magic serves human flourishing.*

Whether that would be enough to defend against the forces arrayed against them remained uncertain. But they would fight, they would do their best to endure, and they would build something better from the ruins.

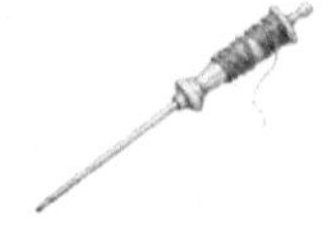

CHAPTER 17
Amara

Pain hauled her back to awareness, sharp and invasive. It wasn't the ache of an injury, but something deeper, spreading from her palms throughout the rest of her body along pathways that felt disturbingly changed. She opened her eyes to a canvas ceiling, morning light seeping through the fabric above. She was in her tent.

The forbidden weave. Memory returned in fragments. Blood-thread and bone, earth folding like cloth, enemies vanishing into silence.

She raised her hands, studying palms that bore marks she'd never seen on living flesh. Not simple burns or cuts, but patterns seared into her skin with the permanence of tattoos. They were thread-shapes that pulsed faintly with their own rhythm, as if the magic she'd woven had become part of her nature rather than something she'd employed and then set aside.

The blisters wept fluid that wasn't clear or bloody, but faintly luminescent, carrying traces of the power. Each throb of pain brought flashes of memory: screams cut short, earth closing with the finality of graves sealed, rebels watching her with mixed expressions ranging from gratitude to horror.

"You wove my will, not yours."

The Weaver's voice threaded through her awareness. He didn't speak from an external source, but the words emerged from someplace inside her consciousness, as if the forbidden technique had strengthened the connections she'd been fighting to weaken.

Was it his will? she wondered, studying the patterns burned into her flesh. *Or mine, shaped by corruption I can no longer distinguish from conscious choice?*

The encampment's atmosphere felt different the moment she stepped outside. Not hostile exactly, but charged with tension. The battlefield had been cleared during the hours she'd slept, bodies removed for burning or burial, but the earth itself bore scars that spoke of magic operating beyond normal boundaries.

Where the Threadbound had been swallowed, the ground showed seamwork—actual stitches visible in stone and soil, as if reality had been treated as fabric and finished accordingly. Beautiful in a horrifying way, proof that her grandmother's teachings had encompassed even dangerous knowledge.

Rebels moved through their morning routines, but they avoided meeting her gaze, their attention sliding away whenever she approached, creating invisible barriers that felt more isolating than physical walls.

A child clutched their mother's leg as Amara passed, whispering words meant to be inaudible but carrying clearly in the morning stillness: "That's her. The one who buried them alive."

The mother's hand moved to cover the child's mouth, but her own expression suggested she shared her child's terror. She was just too polite or too frightened to voice it openly. It wasn't condemnation exactly, but recognition that lines had been crossed, that the person they'd been following had revealed capabilities that resembled their enemies more than it did the savior they'd hoped she might be.

Voices drifted from a cluster of soldiers tending cookfires, voicing their concerns about the battle's conclusion.

"She sealed the earth. Trapped them in stone without trial, without giving them the mercy of a quick death. That's not right. That's Wraithstitcher methods."

"She saved us. The camp would have fallen without that weaving."

"At what cost? How long before she decides we're expendable too? Before she starts sealing dissent along with enemies?"

The arguments continued. They were right to be afraid. She'd used practices that operated beyond the boundaries established to prevent exactly the kind of corruption she'd employed. And part of her, the part that had felt the forbidden weave flow so naturally through her awareness, had wanted to continue. To seal more than just enemies, to reshape reality...

I'm slipping, she understood with crystalline clarity that cut through every rationalization and self-justification. *Between threads of the world, between who I was and what the Weaver wants me to become.*

She returned to her tent and studied the notes she'd made during her grandmother's instruction. They were recorded in a journal whose pages had survived years of careful concealment.

As she looked closer, the ink looked odd. It was darker than she remembered, and when she touched it, her fingers came away stained not with conventional dye but something that looked disturbingly like dried blood.

When did I write this? The handwriting was hers, but she had no memory of transcribing patterns that spoke of earth-weaving, blood-threading, or techniques that treated the boundary between life and death as merely a seam to be worked.

Her hand moved without conscious direction, sketching patterns on blank parchment. The Bone Mirror materialized beneath her fingers—a throne of ivory needles, faceless weavers kneeling in worship, the version of herself that wore power like royal garments.

She watched herself draw it again. And again. Each iteration more detailed than the last, as if practice was bringing her closer to manifesting the vision in physical reality rather than merely depicting it on paper.

Is that a real memory? I remember it, and yet I don't. Am I still me? Or just a vessel they haven't noticed yet? Am I a puppet who thinks she's choosing her own movements while dancing to patterns written by the Weaver?

The thought brought temptation that felt like relief. She could simply leave, abandon the rebellion for their own safety, and remove herself from positions where her corruption might spread to contaminate everyone who looked to her for guidance. Let them find other leaders, people who hadn't crossed lines that couldn't be uncrossed. Let them find someone who didn't feel satisfaction about the compatibility with their nature and the Weaver's vision.

They'd be safer without me, she thought, studying the sketches. *It would be better to have no symbol than one that might transform into their worst enemy.*

———◆———

The assembly gathered without her knowledge, called by Caedric through channels she hadn't been monitoring. Amara remained hidden near her tent's entrance, listening to the voices that carried across the encampment with intentional amplification rather than natural acoustics.

"We stand at a crossroads," Caedric began. "Some of you are afraid. That's reasonable. What you witnessed last night challenges assumptions about the kind of power we're willing to employ."

Movement in the crowd suggested agreement, rebels shifting with the nervous energy of people waiting to see if their concerns would be acknowledged or dismissed.

"But consider this." He raised something that caught the morning light—his old Guild insignia, the mark of authority he'd carried for years before choosing different loyalties. "She could have run. She didn't. She could have let us die. She didn't. And when she could have given in to the dark threads, when that forbidden weave wanted to continue beyond what survival demanded, she stopped herself. That is who she is."

The insignia caught fire in his hand, flames consuming the fabric with an intensity that hinted at accelerants applied beforehand. It was a deliberate ceremony. The destruction of a symbol that represented everything he'd once served.

"I burned my loyalty to the Guild long before today," he continued, letting the flaming remains fall to ground. "If you still follow its Pattern, if you believe institutional authority is preferable to the messy uncertainty of building something different, then leave now. No judgment, no retaliation. There's nothing wrong with wanting different things."

Silence stretched across the assembly. Amara watched through the tent's gap, her heart hammering against her ribs while she waited to see how many would take the offered exit.

A rebel near the front stepped forward, not toward the camp's exit, but into the open space where Caedric stood. He removed a patch from his jacket, the symbol of the Guild certification that marked him as having completed training, and dropped it to the ground beside the burning insignia.

Another followed. Then another. Not everyone. Some melted toward the perimeter, choosing departure over commitment—but enough stayed. Enough to suggest that fear hadn't overcome people's willingness to accept imperfect leaders over systematic oppression.

"If you want to fight for something better," Caedric concluded, his gaze sweeping across the rebels who'd chosen to remain, "follow her. Not because she's perfect or pure or free from corruption's influence. But because she stops herself. Because she bears the weight of power without letting it crush her humanity. Because leadership isn't about moral perfection—it's about enduring the burden without breaking."

<hr>

She found him by the watchfire, his posture revealing his exhaustion. The burned insignia lay in ashes at his feet, the final evidence that bridges to his former life had been destroyed beyond any possibility of reconstruction.

"Thank you," she said, settling beside him with movements that sent pain radiating from her scarred palms. "For what you said. For burning that symbol."

"I meant every word." His attention remained fixed on the flames that danced with the wind. "But you need to understand something. I can't see what you're becoming. I can't predict whether the Weaver's influence will eventually overcome your resistance. All I know is who you are now, in this moment. And that person is worth following."

"You don't know what I felt," she confessed, the words emerging with difficulty. "When the forbidden weave activated, when I felt the earth respond to my will... part of me wanted to keep going. To seal more than enemies. To reshape everything according to a pattern that felt so natural, so right, despite knowing it came from sources I should refuse to trust."

The confession hung between them, seeking absolution she didn't deserve. Not because the impulse had been present, but because some part of her still wanted to accept what the Weaver offered—power sufficient to solve her problems, authority that could impose order on chaos that threatened to consume everything worth preserving.

Caedric studied her burned hands, his gaze tracking the thread-patterns that pulsed with faint luminescence. "You stopped," he said simply. "That's the thread I trust. Not whether you feel temptation—everyone feels that when power is available. It's about whether you choose to act on it when circumstances don't demand such extreme measures."

"And when circumstances do demand it?" she asked, voicing the question that had been building since she'd witnessed her own unconscious sketching. "When the only path requires accepting corruption? When stopping means watching people die who might have been saved by using methods too dangerous to employ?"

"Then we make those choices together," he replied, his hand resting upon hers. "Not you bearing the burden alone while we judge from a safe distance."

The fire flickered as the wind shifted, sending sparks spiraling into the darkness overhead. Their hands remained entwined, a connection that waited to be completed, their intimacy held back.

I love him, she acknowledged. *And he loves me. But speaking it aloud would make it real in ways that feel dangerous when everything else is so uncertain.*

Instead, they sat in silence, watching the flames consume the wood. Leadership wasn't about purity, she understood. It was about making choices that left scars, and refusing to let those scars define everything that came after.

The rebels had chosen to follow her. Not out of fear or compulsion, but through voluntary acceptance. And the Weaver's voice was growing stronger, but so was her conviction that she could forge her own pattern despite every influence that sought to impose different designs.

The burned patterns in her palms pulsed with a gentle rhythm, a permanent reminder that some techniques couldn't be used without cost. But cost and corruption weren't identical, and perhaps learning to distinguish between them was the real test of whether she could lead without becoming the tyrant that bone mirror visions suggested she might become.

"It's time," she said.

"Time for what?" Caedric asked.

"Time to take this war to the gates of the Guild."

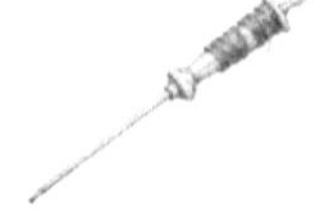

CHAPTER 18
Caedric

The rebel army that gathered on the plains outside Deymar bore little resemblance to the military forces Caedric had commanded during his Guild service. No uniform equipment, no standardized training, no logistics that could support a sustained operation. Just normal people. Farmers carrying pitchforks that had been hastily sharpened into weapons, mercenaries wearing mismatched armor salvaged from a dozen different conflicts, former Guild apprentices who'd turned against masters that had taught them everything they knew about magic and discipline.

This is what revolution actually looks like, he thought, surveying forces that numbered in the hundreds rather than thousands.

He worked with the rebel captains throughout the morning, coordinating flanking teams that would attempt to exploit weaknesses in Guild defensive positions, scouts who would monitor enemy movements and provide early warning of tactical shifts, sappers who'd been trained to undermine fortifications through methods that combined conventional engineering with threadwork that could weaken structural integrity.

But tension radiated through every planning session as doubts about their ability to win became evident. Some people were going through the motions without believing their efforts would prove successful against the Guild forces.

"We can't defeat the Guild's trained soldiers," one captain voiced. "Let alone the Wraithstitchers. We're throwing ourselves against walls that have stood for generations, hoping courage will overcome our disadvantage."

Caedric knew he wasn't wrong. Conventional military assessment suggested their forces were insufficient for the kind of direct confrontation that siege warfare demanded. But conventional assessment missed crucial factors that had shaped conflicts throughout history.

"We don't need to defeat them through superior force," Caedric replied, studying maps that showed Deymar's defensive structures. "We just need to cut the head from the snake."

———◆———

The scouts returned at midday in states of panic, their reports fragmentary and contradictory but consistent on crucial details. The Guild had deployed something new—Stitched Sentinels, woven constructs that moved with an intent that suggested they were driven by more than ordinary enchantment.

"They're not alive," one scout gasped, still trembling from what he'd witnessed. "But they're not dead either. They move, they think, they hunt. And when you cut them, they just... reweave themselves."

Caedric led a small skirmish unit into the forest where the scouts had encountered the Sentinels. The trees grew thick here, their canopy blocking most of the sunlight and creating shadows that could easily conceal enemies until engagement became inevitable.

The first Sentinel emerged from behind an oak trunk with movements that carried unnatural fluidity. It didn't walk so much as flow, fabric forms that maintained humanoid shape through constant small adjustments rather than a fixed structure. Its surface showed patterns that resembled clothing, but the materials pulsed with their own rhythm, as if the construct breathed despite having no lungs or heart.

Caedric's thread-cutter sliced through the fabric with ease. The resistance wasn't like that of flesh or the solid impact of striking armor, but something that parted like water before his blade. But instead of falling, the Sentinel simply reformed, threads reknitting themselves around the damage with a speed that made his attack useless.

They're not just constructs, he realized, watching the thing move toward him. *They retain consciousness. They have human awareness bound into their forms.*

He switched tactics, abandoning attempts to destroy the physical structure in favor of targeting the thread-patterns that animated it. His blade, designed to sever magical connections rather than just cut material, found purchase—each strike disrupting the enchantments.

The Sentinel collapsed, its fabric body losing cohesion. But in the moment before complete dissolution, Caedric heard a voice. Weak and distorted, but recognizably human.

"Please... end this... I can't..."

He recognized the speaker despite the distortion. Garrett, a Hemlock Circle member who'd served in his unit years ago, someone he'd shared watches with during long campaigns, whose family he'd met during leave periods when their professional relationship briefly gave way to genuine friendship.

They're transforming people.

The realization cut deep. The Guild was employing measures that horrified him.

———◆———

During the evening strategy session, someone mentioned the name Master Veylor. Caedric went still. Veylor had trained him how to interrogate people using memory magic that could rewrite what people remembered, leaving no trace of evidence behind.

He was like a second father, Caedric remembered, studying the reports that confirmed Veylor now led the Guild's military contingent outside Deymar. *Someone who believed in me when others saw only a street orphan without proper lineage or connections. He took me under his wing and taught me that service to others was the highest calling any person could embrace.*

But those teachings had been built on foundations too corrupt to support anything worthwhile. Dedication to an authority that sacrificed individual choice in favor of keeping power was tyranny dressed in the language of duty.

He's leading the forces that created the Stitched Sentinels, Caedric realized. *He's helped transform people I once served with into animated weapons. And he believes he's serving the greater good, protecting order from chaos.*

That night, unable to sleep despite his exhaustion, Caedric found himself seeking Amara. She was awake in her tent, studying maps by lamplight. She looked up as he entered, her expression shifting from concentration to concern as she recognized the look of struggle on his face.

"The Guild's field commander is Master Veylor," he said, settling beside her without invitation. "The man who trained me. Who believed in me when no one else did. He shaped my understanding of duty and honor. I don't know if I can fight him, let alone defeat him."

The confession hung between them. He wasn't asking for absolution or advice, just offering the truth about a bond that couldn't be cut cleanly, no matter how rotten its foundations.

Amara didn't speak. She didn't offer platitudes about necessary sacrifices or greater goods that justified personal loss. She simply listened with the kind of attention that made silence enough, then placed her hand over his heart. Not a romantic gesture, just an acknowledgement of the pain he was experiencing.

This was love, he realized, feeling her warmth through the fabric between them. Not grand declarations or heroic gestures—just being present with someone's pain without trying to fix it.

They sat together in silence while lamplight flickered and the distant sounds of camp preparation filtered through canvas walls. Tomorrow he would face someone he once considered family, and the ensuing battle would cut the final thread that tied him to the Guild.

———◆———

Dawn broke. From his position on a ridge overlooking the approach routes, Caedric watched the Guild army deploy from the city. Banners unfurled with patterns designed to intimidate as much as identify—not just military standards, but magical workings as well.

Horns sounded across the valley, their notes carrying harmonics that resonated with enchantments built into the very ground, awakening defenses that had been prepared for exactly this kind of confrontation.

Amara climbed the ridge to stand beside him, her presence offering him comfort.

"There's no turning back," Caedric said.

Below them, the rebel forces moved into positions that would serve as a foundation for their defenses. *The first thread has been cut,* Caedric thought, watching the Guild forces complete their deployment. *Now comes the unraveling.*

Whether that unraveling would lead to victory or destruction remained to be seen. The siege would test everything they were made of. Some would survive, others would fall, and the costs would echo through history regardless of which side won.

But they would face it together. The Threadmarked and her shield, the pattern breaker and her protector, two people bound by choices that couldn't be changed now. The horns sounded again, closer now, marking the beginning of the conflict.

And as the first wave began their advance across the valley floor, Caedric found his hand moving toward his thread-cutter. It wasn't a Guild weapon anymore, but a tool that answered to his will alone.

The fray began with the clash of metal on stone, magic against ward. The threads were fraying, and the time had come to cut them and weave something new from what remained.

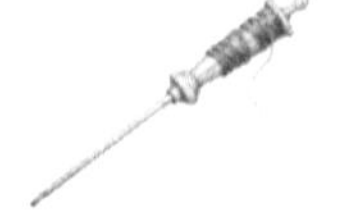

CHAPTER 19
Amara

The morning sun painted Deymar's gates in shades that reminded Amara of blood and fire. Appropriate colors for what was about to unfold. She moved through the rebel lines with purpose, her scarred hands weaving battle-wards into armor, cloaks that bore the stains of previous engagements, even bare skin when soldiers lacked the materials that would normally serve as a foundation for protective enchantments.

Each ward was different, tailored to the individual who would carry it into combat. A child—too young to be here but present nonetheless because war didn't respect innocence—received every defensive pattern Amara knew how to weave. She watched the child's mother clutch them close with gratitude that went beyond words.

The rebellion's standard waited near the command position, its fabric showing wear from being carried through camps and conflicts. She approached it with reverence, knowing that symbols mattered when material advantages were insufficient.

Her hands moved through patterns she'd never been taught, weaving what felt like hope itself into the standard's fabric. Golden thread materialized beneath her fingers—not physical material, but something that manifested by sheer will.

Let them try to unmake this, she thought, watching the golden weave settle into patterns that seemed to catch the light and amplify it. *Let them discover that some things can't be destroyed through force alone.*

Caedric found her as she was completing the final knots. "They fight beside you," he said. "Not because of what you can do, but because of who you are."

The distinction mattered to her. He wasn't following her because she was the Threadmarked, but because of who she was as a person, the person that existed beneath titles and expectations.

The Guild struck first.

Flaming threads lashed from the sky like whips made of concentrated fire, while Stitched Sentinels marched across the fields.

They're not holding back, Amara observed.

She responded with ripple-weaves, enchantments stitched directly into the air itself rather than anchored to physical materials. Invisible until disturbed, they created zones where movement triggered magical responses—threads that cut like razors, patterns that disrupted the animation spells controlling the Sentinels, defensive barriers that materialized only when enemies attempted to pass through marked spaces.

The technique was innovative, but it was also exhausting, requiring constant attention to maintain the delicate balance between potential and manifestation. Each ripple-weave consumed energy that couldn't be recovered until the enchantment was either triggered or deliberately dissolved.

Her cloak flared with power as she channeled magic through patterns woven into its fabric—not just protection, but amplification that let her reach farther, work faster, maintain more simultaneous enchantments than normal limitations would allow. The rebellion's soldiers saw it and took courage, their movements gaining confidence that came from witnessing proof that their side possessed power that could counter Guild advantages.

But every time I channel this deeply, she recognized with growing unease, *I hear the whisper.*

"More. Let me show you how to make this truly effective. Stop limiting yourself to gentle influence when domination would serve better."

The Weaver's voice threaded through her awareness like a needle through yielding fabric, offering techniques that would amplify her effectiveness at costs she was still learning to calculate. Not forcing compliance, but presenting options that felt increasingly reasonable as the battle's intensity mounted.

Just a little more power, the temptation whispered. *Just enough to ensure survival. You can pull back afterward, once the immediate threat is addressed.*

The battle reached its peak as Guild forces committed their reserves, overwhelming defensive positions through sheer numerical advantage that threatened to break through lines that had been holding against impossible odds. Amara watched rebels fall. They weren't abstractions, but people whose names she knew, whose hopes she'd listened to, whose survival mattered to her.

Desperation cut through her careful restraint. *I need to do something, Something that can shift the balance before we lose everything.*

The wide-field pattern emerged from somewhere deep within her consciousness—inherited knowledge that came from sources she'd been trying to reject. A weaving that would unmake thread constructs across the entire battlefield, dissolving the Stitched Sentinels and disrupting Guild enchantments with the efficiency conventional methods couldn't match.

Her hands moved through the pattern's opening gestures before conscious decision could intervene. Power flooded through pathways that had been carved by the forbidden weave she'd used during the night siege, responding in a way that felt natural despite their corrupted origins.

You could accomplish so much more, the Weaver observed with satisfaction that made her stomach clench. *This is merely the beginning of what we could create together.*

For a moment, she saw her reflection in the shimmer of gathering power—eyes darkened to bone-white, fingers skeletal as if the flesh had been stripped away, voice emerging from her throat in harmonics that carried layers belonging to countless others who'd been consumed by her control.

No, she thought. *Not like this. Not at this cost.*

The decision cut through temptation and desperation alike. She could finish the pattern as the Weaver intended, unmake every Guild enchantment on the field and guarantee immediate victory. Or she could choose a different approach—less effective but safer, slower but more aligned with who she was.

Amara shifted the weaving mid-pattern, redirecting power into channels that required more effort but didn't draw on sources that would strengthen the tether's influence. Not unmaking everything, but creating zones where Guild magic failed while rebel enchantments remained functional. It wasn't domination, but the advantage that came from superior practice rather than overwhelming force.

The enemy was pushed back, their assault losing coordination as critical enchantments failed and Stitched Sentinels collapsed. But the strain nearly destroyed her. Channeling that much power while trying to control it was proving to be too much. Every instinct screamed to accept the easier alternatives that corruption offered.

She collapsed as the pattern completed, her consciousness threatening to fragment under the pressure. She'd pushed her gift beyond its limits, further than ever before. Her body trembled, and sweat seemed to come from every pore of her flesh. It was all she could do to breathe. Her strength slowly returned and she stood.

Victory felt hollow as Amara surveyed the aftermath. Dozens of rebels lay among the fallen—some dead, others injured in ways that might prove fatal despite the healers' best efforts. The Stitched Sentinels had been destroyed but needed burning before their materials could be reconstructed.

She stood beside the funeral pyres as they were lit, whispering apologies to the souls that had been trapped within the constructed forms. Each fire felt like a confession—not of guilt for their deaths, but that the freedom she'd given them had come through destruction rather than genuine liberation.

I couldn't save them, the truth cut deeper than any physical wound. *I just ended their suffering by eliminating what they'd been transformed into.*

Caedric joined her on the battlefield, her hands trembling from magical exhaustion.

"Every stitch I pull to save them," she said, her voice barely above a whisper, "brings me closer to something I don't want to become. The Weaver was right there, in my head, showing me how to win. And part of me wanted to accept what he offered."

He took her hands in his, and the scarred patterns in her palms pulsed against his skin, feeling warmth that had nothing to do with magical exertion.

"I won't let you face the darkness alone."

The words were still settling between them when a commotion arose near the perimeter. Amara turned to see two scouts dragging a prisoner toward the command tent. A man in Guild robes, his hands bound with suppression threads that glowed faintly in the firelight.

"War-weaver," one of the scouts reported. "Found him trying to slip through our lines during the chaos. He was carrying schematics."

Caedric's expression hardened. "The Guild doesn't send war-weavers on solo reconnaissance. He was left behind deliberately—either as a spy or because he knows something they don't want captured."

Amara looked at the prisoner. Even restrained and defeated, he held himself with the rigid composure of someone who'd spent years in Guild service. His eyes met hers briefly, then slid away, his dismissal making it obvious he believed her to be beneath his notice.

"Take him to the command tent," she said. "I'll question him after the pyres have finished burning."

But as the scouts led him away, she felt the Weaver's presence stir at the edges of her consciousness. He was interested, eager even, at the prospect of what secrets might be extracted from a captured Guild operative.

She pushed the whisper aside and turned back to the fires, watching until the last of the Stitched Sentinels had been reduced to ash. The dead deserved her full attention in their final moments, not a divided focus on what strategic advantage might come next.

When the flames had finally died and the survivors had begun the grim work of identifying bodies, Amara made her way to the command tent. Caedric fell into step beside her, and she was grateful for his presence.

The captured war-weaver was waiting in the command tent, his restraints woven from threads that would prevent magical working while allowing normal movement. He refused to speak despite questioning that ranged from gentle inquiry to threats of consequences that would mirror what the Guild had done to create their Stitched Sentinels.

He won't respond to conventional interrogation, Amara knew, studying eyes that held the kind of devotion that came from decades of institutional conditioning. *His loyalty runs too deep, reinforced to ensure coercion is ineffective.*

But she'd learned memory-threading from her grandmother, whose knowledge predated Guild standardization. She couldn't read minds in the conventional sense, but she could follow threads of recollection to find knowledge that subjects might not consciously access.

Her hands moved through patterns that felt simultaneously familiar and foreign, threading consciousness to consciousness to create a temporary bridge between separate minds. It wasn't a forceful connection, but instead allowed her to access information the prisoner carried without realizing its significance.

Images flooded her awareness—not organized thoughts, but fragments of experience that had shaped his understanding of what the Guild represented and what purposes his service supported.

A chamber deep beneath Deymar, its walls lined with looms that had been carved from bone rather than constructed from wood or metal. Threadwork that pulsed with its own rhythm, patterns that predated not just the Guild but the original settlements that had become cities. Power that existed independent of human will or conscious direction, ancient beyond measurement and terrible in its implications.

The Weaver of Bone's origin, she understood with growing horror. *Not a metaphorical connection, but the actual source—the place where he was created.*

And woven through the vision, glimpses of a tapestry that matched fragments she'd been carrying since their flight from the Bone Cloister. The prophecy that had marked cities for destruction, that had identified her as significant to the conflict.

The final piece, she realized. *Whatever answers exist about the tether, about what I'm becoming, about how to resist the corruption that grows stronger with each weaving—it's there.*

She broke the connection, exhaustion threatening to overwhelm her. The war-weaver collapsed, his mind retreating from the contact that had exposed knowledge he'd been conditioned to protect with his life.

I know where to go, she thought, studying the mental map that memory-threading had revealed. *I know what I'm looking for and why the Guild has been so desperate to prevent us from reaching the Looming Gate.*

But this knowledge had a price beyond exhaustion. Each time she used her gift, the tether's grip tightened, carving channels that let corruption flow more easily into her mind. The Weaver had been present during the battle—not just watching, but participating, showing her methods that proved increasingly difficult to distinguish from her own intuitions.

How much longer can I resist? How many more battles before the distinction between who I am and what he wants me to become dissolves entirely?

They would need to plan the assault on Deymar in a way that the rebels would draw the attention of the Guild so she could find a way to the chamber beneath the Guild Hall. It wouldn't be easy, especially with the losses they'd suffered. But it was possible.

She would find the Weaver of Bone, and she would destroy him.

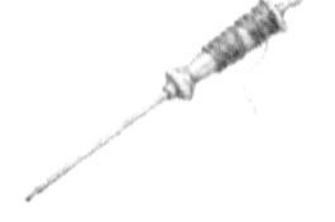

CHAPTER 20
Caedric

The passage descended through layers of stone that predated Deymar's visible architecture, each level revealing construction methods from civilizations that had risen and fallen before the Guild claimed authority over how magic should be practiced.

Amara led the small group—Maela, two former Guild defectors whose knowledge of the citadel's layout had proven invaluable, and three rebels whose loyalty had been tested through several battles.

This is where it began, she understood, studying the carved symbols in the walls, symbols that resembled threadwork. *This is where the first Weavers discovered the power, where someone decided that such power required control rather than leaving it in the hands of ordinary people who might use it for something other than conquest.*

The Bone Chamber announced itself through sensation before sight. It came as pressure building against her awareness like an approaching storm, threads that existed independent of physical material humming with frequencies that resonated with the scars on her palms. The passage opened into a space that was vast beyond normal architecture and filled with looms that spun without human touch.

The looms were carved from bone rather than constructed from wood or metal, their surfaces marked with patterns that pulsed with their own rhythm. Threads stretched between posts that rose toward a ceiling lost in darkness overhead, creating webs that generated their own bone-white luminescence. It wasn't reflected light, but something cold and unnatural—death transformed into a tool.

Echoes, she realized, studying the shadows. They moved with purpose, more than merely an absence of light. They were remnants of those who'd been consumed by the power they thought to control. All of them wore bone-threaded cloaks.

A tapestry dominated the chamber's center, larger than any she'd encountered, its patterns showing futures that remained unwoven—potential rather than certainty, possibilities that existed because choices had not yet been made. One thread showed her sitting on a throne of ivory needles, her eyes like shadowed glass, power radiating from her form while faceless masses knelt in worship.

Caedric

The Guild's final assault came with everything they had remaining: elite units that had been held in reserve for exactly this kind of desperate defense, Wraithstitchers who'd been given permission to employ practices normally forbidden even by their own standards, war-weavers whose enchantments could reshape the battlefield itself.

They know what she's attempting below, Caedric realized, studying the attack patterns that pointed to a singular focus. *They know that if she succeeds, everything the Guild represents will cease to exist. And they're willing to sacrifice everything to prevent that outcome.*

He fought alongside former Hemlock Circle members who'd defected after witnessing what their service actually accomplished, commonfolk who'd taken up weapons despite having no military training, rebels who wielded wards that Amara had stitched before descending into the chamber. It wasn't an organized army in any conventional sense, but people who'd chosen to stand together despite every force that sought to separate them.

The wards proved more effective than anyone had anticipated—not just for protection, but offensive capabilities that emerged when defenders channeled their own determination through the patterns Amara had designed, allowing them to respond to user intent rather than following fixed programming. Shields that could strike, barriers that could trap, defensive enchantments that transformed into weapons when circumstances demanded it.

She's still protecting us, he realized, watching a farmer whose ward had just saved him from a killing blow. *Even while facing what waits below, she's present in the magic she left behind.*

Master Veylor emerged from the Guild ranks, and Caedric's breath caught. The man who'd shaped everything he'd once believed himself to be. Who'd taught him that sacrifice for the Guild was the highest calling, that duty meant putting aside personal desire for the greater good. The same man who'd once sat vigil with him through three nights when Caedric had nearly failed his final trial, speaking quiet words about honor and purpose until Caedric found the strength to continue.

The man who'd been more of a father to him than his own blood had ever managed now stood against him. The grief hit him like a physical blow, stealing the air from his lungs.

He genuinely believes he's on the right side.

They faced each other across ground churned to mud by magic and blood. Teacher and student. Father figure and son. Their paths had diverged toward destinations so different that they couldn't be reconciled through anything except one side's complete defeat.

Caedric's hand tightened on his thread-cutter, and the familiar weight of it suddenly felt wrong. The blade had been a gift from Veylor on the day he'd completed his training. *"May it serve truth and honor all your days,"* he had said, his voice thick with the pride that Caedric had desperately wanted to deserve.

"You could have been great," Veylor said, and the disappointment in his voice cut deeper than any weapon. It was the tone he'd used when Caedric had failed a lesson, when he'd shown weakness or questioned orders—but magnified a hundredfold. "You could have led the Hemlock Circle, helped shape policy for generations. Instead, you chose betrayal for a woman whose corruption will destroy everything we've built."

The words landed like blows, each one finding the vulnerable places Caedric had tried to armor against. Part of him—the part that had spent seven years seeking Veylor's approval, that had pushed himself to exhaustion trying to be worthy of that rare praise—wanted to defend himself, to explain that he hadn't chosen betrayal, that the Guild itself had betrayed everything it claimed to represent.

But the explanation died unspoken. Veylor wouldn't hear it. Couldn't hear it. His conviction was absolute, forged through decades of service into something unshakeable.

"You taught me to question," Caedric said finally, and was dismayed to hear his voice crack slightly. "To look beneath the surface, to find the truth that others tried to hide. I did exactly what you trained me to do."

"I taught you to question *others*," Veylor replied, and there was genuine pain beneath the steel in his tone. "Not the foundations that give your questions meaning. You were like a son to me, Caedric. Losing you..." He paused, and for just a moment, the perfect control wavered. "It would have been kinder if you'd simply died."

Caedric felt something break inside him. Not his resolve, but the last fragile hope that somehow, impossibly, this could end without one of them destroying what the other had become.

Veylor moved first, his hands tracing patterns in the air with fluid precision. Threads of compulsion shot toward Caedric—not physical bindings, but constructs designed to rewrite thought itself. The weave was elegant, devastating, exactly the kind of technique Veylor had perfected over decades: invisible chains that would make Caedric *want* to obey, that would reshape his motivations until betraying Amara felt like the only honorable choice.

Caedric's thread-cutter sang through the air, severing the connections before they could take hold. But Veylor had anticipated the defense—he always did. The compulsion threads weren't the real attack, just a feint to draw out Caedric's response and expose his positioning.

The true strike came from below, threads erupting from the churned mud like serpents. They wrapped around Caedric's ankles, burning cold where they touched flesh. Memory-bindings, designed to pull him back into the mindset of an obedient enforcer. He could feel them tugging at his thoughts, whispering that the Guild was right, that his defection had been madness, that everything Veylor said was—

He severed the threads with a savage downward cut, stumbling back. His breath came hard. Three seconds into the fight and Veylor had already breached his defenses twice.

"You're hesitating," Veylor said, circling left. His hands moved in constant motion, weaving new patterns even as he spoke. "That's always been your weakness—you *feel* too much. Sentiment clouds your judgment."

Caedric didn't answer. Words were weapons in Veylor's arsenal, designed to distract while his true attack took shape. He could see it forming now—a lattice of oath-threads, the same technique used to bind recruits to Guild service, but amplified to crushing intensity. If those threads found purchase, they would lock Caedric's will in chains that couldn't be broken without shattering his mind entirely.

He shifted his stance, pulling on techniques Veylor had never seen because he'd learned them after his defection. Amara had shown him how to weave defensively, creating barriers that didn't just block but redirected—turning an attacker's power back on itself.

The oath-threads struck his barrier and tangled, their compulsion folding inward. Veylor's eyes widened fractionally—the first genuine surprise Caedric had ever seen him show in combat.

"New tricks," the old man acknowledged. His tone held grudging respect beneath the disappointment. "She's been teaching you. Corrupting everything I built in you."

"She's been teaching me to think for myself." Caedric pressed forward, his thread-cutter carving through the space between them. The blade found Veylor's defensive weave and sliced it apart, forcing the older man back a step.

But Veylor recovered instantly, his hands blurring through a pattern Caedric recognized with cold dread. Memory extraction—the technique used during interrogations to pull knowledge directly from a subject's mind. Veylor wasn't trying to control him anymore. He was trying to *take* what Caedric knew about the resistance, about Amara's plans, about everything that might help the Guild crush what remained of their opposition.

The threads lanced toward Caedric's temple, impossibly fast. He twisted, felt one graze his cheek—and suddenly he was seven years younger, standing in the Guild Hall, swearing his oath of service while Veylor watched with pride that had made Caedric's chest swell with purpose.

The memory wasn't his own. It was Veylor's, reflected back through the extraction attempt. A moment the old man had treasured, held close all these years.

He genuinely loved me, Caedric realized, even as his blade found the memory thread and severed it. *This is killing him as surely as it's killing me.*

But sentiment was a luxury neither of them could afford. Veylor struck again, and again, each attack more desperate than the last. Compulsion gave way to memory-bindings which gave way to raw will-breaking force—techniques that would leave permanent damage even if they failed to achieve their immediate purpose.

Caedric met each strike with defenses that were barely adequate, feeling his strength beginning to flag. Veylor had decades more experience, deeper reserves, and the absolute conviction that made his magic burn brighter. The only advantage Caedric possessed was knowledge his teacher lacked—techniques learned outside Guild orthodoxy, patterns that didn't fit the rigid structure of institutional magic.

He wove shadows the way Amara had shown him, not blocking Veylor's next attack but making it *uncertain* where the real target stood. The old man's threads struck empty air while Caedric circled behind, his blade aimed at the binding points that powered Veylor's defenses.

One cut. Two. The third caught something vital, and Veylor's entire weave collapsed inward with a sound like tearing silk.

The old man staggered, his perfect control finally breaking. Blood ran from his nose— backlash from severed connections. His hands trembled as he tried to rebuild his defenses, but the damage was too severe, the opening too wide.

Caedric stood over him, thread-cutter raised for the killing strike. All he had to do was sever one more connection and it would be over.

"Go," Caedric said, offering mercy. "Find somewhere the Guild's authority doesn't reach. Build something better from what remains."

A Guild blade caught him as he turned away from his defeated mentor, pain exploding through his side where the armor had been compromised. The blow wasn't fatal, not yet, but if left untreated, it would be his end. He positioned himself in front of the passage that led to the Bone Chamber.

I just need to hold them back until she finishes, he thought.

Amara

The air in the chamber split open like torn fabric, and the Weaver of Bone stepped through.

Reality itself recoiled from his presence. The bone-white threads suspended throughout the vast space began to hum—a sound that vibrated in Amara's teeth, her bones, the silver scars carved into her flesh. He was tall, impossibly skeletal, wrapped in robes that didn't just absorb light but *devoured* it, leaving wounds in the air where illumination had been.

But he was also different from her visions. More and less than she'd expected. His form flickered between solid and spectral, half-spirit and half-cloth, held together by fragments of countless souls he'd consumed over centuries. She could see them shifting beneath his skin like shadows under ice—faces pressed against the inside of his being, mouths open in silent screams.

Beautiful, in the way a blade was beautiful. Terrible in the way an avalanche was terrible—natural, inevitable, and completely indifferent to what it destroyed.

"Amara." Her name in his mouth sounded wrong, like hearing a beloved song played on instruments made from human bone. "You've come so far. Learned so much. Accepted what others called forbidden." The bone runes beneath her skin began to burn, responding to harmonics in his voice that resonated with the corruption he'd planted in her. "All that remains is the final step—accepting what you were always meant to become."

He gestured, and the world *changed.*

The vision didn't just appear before her—it crashed over her like a wave, pulling her under into possibility made manifest. She saw herself standing above a world remade. Cities where perfect order replaced chaos, where every thread of existence wove according to predetermined patterns, where suffering had been systematically eliminated because choice itself had been removed. Peace, finally. True peace.

And it was glorious. Pattern help her, it was glorious.

The power sang in her veins. The ability to reshape civilization with a thought, to impose harmony on discord, to *fix* everything that was broken about the world. No more war. No more pain. No more desperate struggles to overcome. Just perfect, eternal order.

All it costs is who you are, something whispered in the deepest part of her consciousness. *Everything that makes you... you.*

The Weaver moved closer, and his hands reached toward her. Where they touched, her spirit began to unravel. She could feel her individual consciousness beginning to dissolve, merging into something larger, grander, freed from the messy limitations of personal desire.

"You see now," he said, and his voice was gentle, almost loving. "How small you've been. How confined by flesh and fear and the illusion of choice."

For a heartbeat—two—three—she was tempted.

Because he was right. The vision of peace through obedience, control through order, the systematic elimination of suffering through removal of everything that made suffering possible—it made *sense*. Perfect, crystalline, irrefutable sense. And she was so tired. So exhausted from carrying the weight of thousands of lives on her shoulders, from making choices that killed people she'd promised to protect, from watching the world burn while she struggled to find answers that didn't exist.

How easy it would be to just... surrender. To let go. To become part of something that promised to fix everything.

The bone runes flared brighter, and she felt herself beginning to slip—

No.

The thought came from somewhere deeper than conscious decision. A place the Weaver's corruption hadn't reached, couldn't reach, because it was the essential core of what made her herself.

The loom doesn't weave peace. It weaves fear.

Clarity crashed through her like shattering glass. She saw past the beautiful vision to what lay beneath: peace purchased through the murder of human will itself.

"No," she said, and the word emerged with conviction that surprised her. Power blazed along the silver scars in her arms as she tore herself free from the Weaver's unraveling touch. "I've seen what you're offering. Watched it take shape in the bone mirror visions and forbidden weaves that felt too natural, too right. And I refuse."

The Weaver's expression didn't change—she wasn't certain he had expressions in any conventional sense—but the air around him grew colder, heavier, pressing down with the weight of his displeasure.

"You refuse," he repeated, and now his voice carried harmonics that made her bones ache. "You, who are already half-transformed. Who bear my mark in your flesh. Who have tasted the power I offer and found it sweet." He gestured, and the souls trapped within him writhed visibly. "You think you have a choice, child? You became mine the moment you first accepted my gift. Every stitch you've pulled since then has only drawn you deeper into patterns you cannot escape."

"You're right," Amara said, the truth settling around her shoulders like armor. "I can't escape what I've become. The corruption is part of me now, woven so deep that cutting it out would mean destroying myself." She raised her hands, and the bone runes blazed with silver light—not his bone-white luminescence, but something that belonged to her alone. "But that doesn't mean I have to let it control me. I choose what I become. Not you. Not the Guild. Not prophecy or destiny. *Me*."

For the first time since materializing, the Weaver of Bone looked genuinely surprised.

"Impossible," he breathed. "No one has ever—"

"Then I'll be the first."

Caedric

Caedric stumbled back, his boots slipping in blood—his own and others'—that had turned the stone floor treacherous. His thread-cutter felt impossibly heavy in his hand, the enchanted blade's glow dimming as his strength failed. Around him, rebel defenders formed a ragged line, their faces masks of exhaustion and terror and desperate, stubborn refusal to break.

Guild forces crashed against them like waves against a crumbling seawall.

Just hold, Caedric thought, blocking a strike that sent shockwaves up his arm. *Just a little longer.*

His vision swam. Blood loss was making the world distant, sounds reaching him as if through deep water. Pain had transformed from immediate sensation into abstract concept—he knew he was wounded, badly, but the specifics seemed unimportant compared to the simple fact that he was still standing, still fighting, still keeping the Guild's elite units from reaching the chamber where Amara faced the Weaver alone.

A war-weaver broke through on his left. Caedric pivoted, too slow, knowing he wouldn't reach the threat in time. But one of the rebel defenders—a young woman whose name he'd never learned—threw herself into the gap, her crude spear finding the war-weaver's throat even as his enchanted blade carved through her chest.

She fell without a sound, and Caedric kept fighting.

Some things are worth dying to protect.

The thought came with crystalline clarity, cutting through the fog of blood loss and exhaustion. Not the abstract principles he'd once served in the Guild, not institutional mandates or carefully constructed justifications. Just this: the woman he loved, facing a horror beyond mortal comprehension, trusting him to keep the wolves at bay while she fought for the world's soul.

He could do that. Even dying, he could do that much.

"Push forward!" a voice cut through the chaos. "They're breaking! One more assault and—"

The ground trembled, and the fighting paused. The air itself began to shimmer, and through the passage leading deeper into the fortress, silver light blazed.

She's doing it, he realized. *It's happening now.*

Amara

The cutthread pattern her grandmother had taught her was simple in principle, near impossible in execution. It was a weaving designed to sever the weaver from the weave itself, to eliminate the connection between consciousness and the power that had defined existence for longer than anyone could remember.

It will end magic as we understand it, she knew, beginning the pattern with hands that trembled from exhaustion and fear in equal measure. *The Pattern will be fragmented beyond anyone's ability to dominate it again. I will make it weak and scattered, reduce it to thread-memory, incapable of being wielded by anyone that would use it to impose control.*

The moment her threads found their first binding point, the Weaver *screamed.*

Not rage—she'd expected rage. This was sorrow. Pure, devastating grief as he recognized what was being unmade. The sound reverberated through the chamber, through the fortress, through reality itself, and souls trapped within his form began to break free, streaming upward like smoke finally released after centuries of compression.

"You don't understand what you're destroying!" His form flickered, already beginning to unravel as the pattern took hold. "Not just me, but the legacy of everyone who contributed to this power. The accumulated wisdom of centuries, techniques that let humanity transcend its limitations, the possibility of shaping reality according to human vision rather than accepting what nature provides—"

"I understand!" Amara's voice cracked like thunder, and power blazed along every silver scar on her body. She wove faster, the pattern growing more complex with each pass of her hands. "I understand that some legacies are too corrupt to preserve! That wisdom which eliminates human agency isn't wisdom—it's oppression dressed in scholarly robes! Power which demands this much suffering isn't worth any benefit it provides!"

The bone-white threads throughout the chamber began to snap, releasing voices that had been compressed into infrastructure. The walls themselves started to crack, ancient stone unable to withstand the dissolution of magic that had held it together for generations.

The Weaver lunged toward her, desperation overriding his dignified sorrow. His hands—those terrible, beautiful hands—reached for the pattern she was weaving, trying to tear it apart before completion.

But she'd learned from him. Every forbidden technique, every corruption he'd planted in her consciousness—she turned it all against him now.

Her grandmother's teachings. The prophecy fragments she'd carried since the Bone Cloister. The love she felt for Caedric and the people who'd died trusting her to find another way. All of it wove together into something that had never existed before: a pattern that belonged entirely to her, that drew on corruption without being consumed by it, that wielded power while simultaneously destroying the possibility of domination.

The cutthread found its final binding point.

Reality screamed as the connection severed.

The Weaver came apart like fabric being unstitched from existence itself. His form lost cohesion, dissolving into thousands of individual threads that had once been souls, knowledge, accumulated power condensed across centuries. They spiraled upward through the collapsing chamber, finally free, finally able to dissipate into natural patterns instead of serving another's will.

For just a moment, she saw him clearly—not the monster he'd become, but what he might have been before corruption. A weaver. A teacher. Someone who'd discovered something profound and then spent an eternity perverting it.

I'm sorry, she thought, even as she maintained the pattern that was destroying him. *For whatever you were before this. For the knowledge being lost. For everything that might have been preserved if only it hadn't been so thoroughly entangled with domination.*

But sorrow didn't mean regret. Some things needed ending, even when ending them meant losing what might never be recovered.

The Bone Chamber shattered.

The ancient looms exploded outward, their frames dissolving as the magic sustaining them returned to raw potential that no single consciousness could claim. The floor cracked open, revealing chasms that dropped into darkness beyond measurement. The ceiling collapsed, massive stones falling where Amara had stood moments before.

She ran.

Ran through passages that were tearing themselves apart, through air thick with released magic that burned against her skin, through screaming reality as the fundamental laws that had governed this place for centuries rewrote themselves into chaos. Behind her, the Bone Chamber imploded completely, its secrets buried beneath tons of rubble that would never yield them to anyone who might attempt reconstruction.

The passage ahead blazed with daylight, impossibly bright after the darkness. She burst into the open air and stumbled, her legs finally giving out, unable to carry her another step. The world spun. Her consciousness flickered like a candle in high wind.

Strong arms caught her before she hit the ground.

Caedric. Barely upright himself, blood soaking through his armor from a dozen wounds, swaying like a tree in a storm, but alive. Breathing. Present when she needed him most.

"It's done," she gasped, clutching at him, needing the solid reality of his presence to anchor her against the vertigo of what she'd just accomplished. "The Weaver is unmade. The Guild's power is broken. Magic itself has been—"

He kissed her.

His lips found hers with desperate tenderness, tasting of blood and salt and relief so profound it bordered on pain. The kiss said everything words couldn't.

Around them, the battle had stopped. Guild forces and rebels alike stood frozen, watching the city of Deymar collapse in on itself, feeling the fundamental shift in reality as magic transformed from tool of domination into something wild and ungovernable.

When they finally broke apart, Amara pressed her forehead against Caedric's, drawing strength from his presence even as she lent him her own.

"It's over," she whispered. "We're free."

Dust rose in massive clouds, obscuring the ruins of everything the Weaver had built.

And in that dust, in the settling debris, was the shocked silence of thousands of people trying to comprehend what had just changed.

EPILOGUE

Six months after the Bone Chamber's fall, the changes were undeniable. The Guild had collapsed—not through military conquest, but through quiet dissolution as its foundational authority simply ceased to exist. One by one, Guild Halls across the realm closed their doors. Some were repurposed into schools or community centers. Others stood empty, monuments to a vision of order that the world had outgrown.

Cities flourished in the absence of institutional oversight. Communities discovered they didn't require distant authorities dictating how they should live, what they should believe, how they should organize their daily existence. Councils formed—messy, argumentative, gloriously chaotic gatherings where people with wildly different perspectives somehow found ways to coexist and compromise and build something together.

It wasn't perfect. Nothing created by imperfect beings ever was. But it was *theirs*, and that made all the difference.

Stitching magic remained, but it was different. Memory fragments could be woven into useful enchantments, healing salves, and protective wards, but it was no longer capable of reshaping reality.

The power had returned to itself, scattered like seeds across fertile ground, growing wild and beautiful and free.

Amara and Caedric traveled through these transformed regions, not as leaders, but as people in love who'd finally earned the right to a normal existence. They didn't seek attention or authority. They wanted only the freedom to build a life together.

In a village nestled in a valley whose name didn't appear on any map they'd consulted, they stopped to rest. The marketplace bustled with familiar energy—merchants hawking wares, children dodging between cart wheels, the comfortable chaos of community going about its daily business.

A little girl ran past, no more than five or six years old, clutching a stitched doll against her chest. The toy was a simple, crude construction, made of mismatched fabric scraps and one button eye slightly higher than the other. There was nothing special about it. Nothing powerful or profound.

And yet, for just a moment, Amara heard it hum.

Not the bone-deep resonance of ancient power. Not the terrible weight of souls compressed into infrastructure. Just a gentle vibration that spoke of life and joy and the simple pleasure of creation that served no purpose except making someone happy.

It's still there, she thought, watching the child disappear around a corner, her laughter trailing behind like music. *Changed and fragmented, scattered and wild—but present. Growing in ways we never could have planned.*

"You're smiling," Caedric observed, his hand finding hers, fingers intertwining in a gesture that had become as natural as breathing.

"I'm happy," she said, and realized with wonder that it was true. Completely, genuinely true in a way she hadn't been sure she'd ever feel again.

Around them, the market continued its business. A young weaver—no older than Amara had been when this all began—sat at a stall, creating enchanted cloth that would keep its owner warm through winter. An elderly man bargained for thread-bound bandages that would speed healing. A mother examined children's clothes that had been stitched with protective wards to keep them safe from common accidents.

Magic in service of daily life. Power used not to dominate, but to help.

"Look," Caedric said softly, nodding toward the village square.

A monument stood there, recently erected. A loom, carved from pale stone, with an inscription beneath it that read: *We weave our own patterns now.*

Amara felt tears prick her eyes, but they were good tears. Healing tears.

The world had been unraveled. And now, thread by thread, stitch by patient stitch, people were weaving something better from what remained. It wouldn't be perfect. There would be struggles, setbacks, moments when the old temptations of easy answers and imposed order beckoned seductively. But that was the price of freedom—the constant work of choosing it, again and again, in moments small and large.

"Where to next?" Caedric asked, though his tone suggested he didn't particularly care as long as they went together.

Amara looked at the road stretching beyond the village, winding through fields where spring flowers were beginning to bloom. She thought of all the places they might go, all the communities finding their own way forward, all the small moments of magic and joy and ordinary wonder waiting to be discovered.

"Wherever we want," she said. "We have time now. All the time in the world."

THE END

About the Author

Richard Fierce is a fantasy author with a passion for storytelling that dates back to his childhood. He first ventured into publishing in 2007 and hasn't looked back since. His books are filled with dragons, adventure, and the kind of epic journeys that transport readers to new worlds.

In 2000, Richard was named Poet of the Year for his poem The Darkness, and his love for literature extends beyond just writing—he co-founded the Acworth Book Festival in Georgia to help bring authors and readers together. Though he originally worked in retail, he eventually transitioned to the tech industry, balancing his career with his writing.

Richard lives in Northwest Georgia with his family and a lively mix of pets, including four dogs (huskies!). He often jokes that his house feels like a zoo, but he wouldn't have it any other way.

His love for fantasy started in high school when he was gifted a copy of *Dragons of Spring Dawning* by Margaret Weis and Tracy Hickman—a book that sparked a lifelong love for dragons and epic quests.